MIRACLE of LIGHT

MIRACLE of LIGHT

ARCHIVES OF THE WARDEN
A Novella of DeVerre

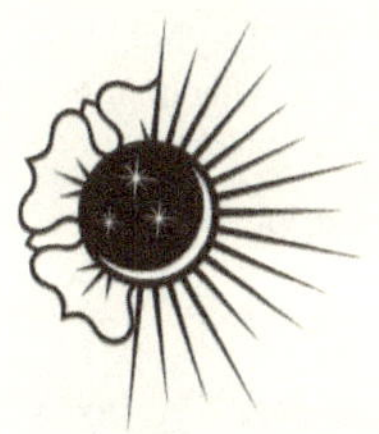

V. K. DIXON

XHP
xenia house press

For my favorite holiday,
and what it means to me

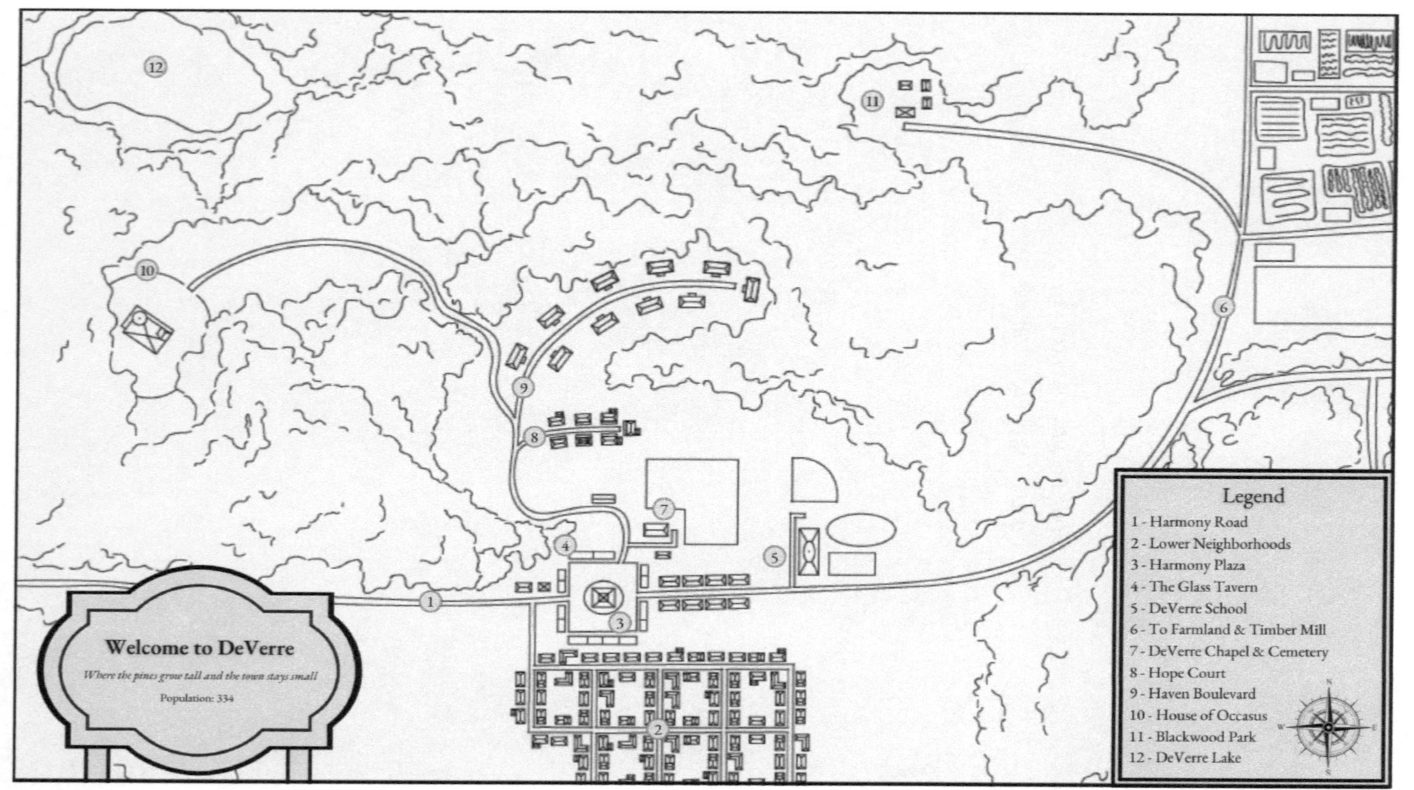

Legend
1 - Harmony Road
2 - Lower Neighborhoods
3 - Harmony Plaza
4 - The Glass Tavern
5 - DeVerre School
6 - To Farmland & Timber Mill
7 - DeVerre Chapel & Cemetery
8 - Hope Court
9 - Haven Boulevard
10 - House of Occasus
11 - Blackwood Park
12 - DeVerre Lake
Welcome to DeVerre
Where the pines grow tall and the town stays small
Population: 334

Table of Contents

Author's Note

The spirit world referenced in this novel is inspired by the truth.
It is not, however, the real truth.
In making the truth fantastic, it is my hope to stir up questions within reality.

Previously in

ARCHIVES OF THE WARDEN

Two months ago . . .

Upon an unexpected inheritance, brothers and co-authors Peter and Spencer Collins moved to the small town of DeVerre, Washington, to accept the grand estate of their estranged great-aunt, Diane Larkin, and pursue their lifelong dream of being full-time authors. Along with their inheritance of a new house—called the House of Occasus—two dogs, and the townspeople's suspicions, they found themselves drawn into the mysterious past of their great-aunt and the reason for her move to DeVerre over thirty years ago.

With the help of Diane's closest friend, Cassandra Clement—who, to their surprise, was a young and attractive woman their own age—the brothers discovered that they were not biological Collins as they believed. Their ancestors originated from DeVerre. Cassandra taught them about Diane's search for the parents she'd lost and introduced them to the spirit world that the two women had discovered together. A world filled with ghosts, phantoms, and beasts.

Together, the trio sought out the truth of the brothers' past and the secrets held in the town. Their pursuit of answers led them to Owen Bernard, a Wielder of the spirit world and agent of the Warden sent to DeVerre to ensure its safety. Owen taught them about the Warden—an organization dedicated to protecting the spirit world from the machinations of the Druids—and about the Veil hidden within DeVerre—a space where the line between the spirit world and physical world was thinnest.

As a team of four, Peter, Spencer, Cassandra, and Owen discovered the presence of Druids within the town, working to take over the Veil. Their investigation led them to the discovery that Cassandra's cousin,

Debbie Mercier, was one of these Druids intent on taking control of the Veil.

Through weeks of trial and error and two near-death run-ins with the Druids, they finally found the key to the secrets they were so desperate to uncover. The brothers learned that they were Varons and discovered a list with the names of the Druids within DeVerre.

Armed with the knowledge, they prepared to rid the town of Druids. But before they could enact their plan, the cultists attacked their home, twenty against four. Only through a feat of extreme, unknown power did Cassandra drive the Druids back, saving their lives.

After their survival, the team prepared to face the remaining threat of Druids in their town, desperate to earn the townspeople's trust. However, before they could convince the town of anything, Peter stumbled upon a meeting with the Druid leader, Alexander Frossard. Unable to get away in time, Alexander took Peter captive.

Spencer was desperate to find his missing brother. Along with their friends, Spencer, Cassandra, and Owen worked to stop the Druids and save Peter, even bringing in Silas Varon, a distant relative of the brothers. But the Druids had a firmer hold on the town than they'd ever realized.

Fighting the leadership of the town, Spencer was stalled in recovering his brother, leaving Peter the captive of Alexander Frossard, subject to the thrall of a valravn, a bird-like beast with the power to manipulate the mind. For four days, Peter was subjected to nightmares, watching Spencer die and hearing his family call for his help. Suddenly, his dreams began to change when a raven interrupted the nightmares, bringing the visage of a mysterious redhead with it.

After being freed by Connor Frossard, Alexander's son, ready to throw off his father's abusive control, Peter was returned to Spencer and Occasus. With Connor's help, they prepared to bring down the Druids before they could enact their ultimate plans within DeVerre: Unleashing the Spectral from the Veil.

In the midst of their planning, Silas revealed to Peter that he was the "true Varon" of Matthias's line, marking him as the primary leader of the Varon bloodline. They also learned that Cassandra was a potential Vessel, a wielder of extraordinary power that the Druids wanted to control.

In a battle at the lake, the brothers and their friends fought to stop the Druids, but while they removed the Vessel prepared by the Druids to house the Spectral, they couldn't stop them from tearing the Veil. The Spectral was freed, the Druids forfeiting their lives in a fight to take Cassandra, the presumed Vessel.

With the removal of the Druids from DeVerre, the town was presumably safe and back under Warden control.

A month later, we return to the grieving and recovering Varon brothers, Cassandra, and DeVerreans at the start of Christmas week . . .

CHAPTER ONE

Peter

The crystalline lake glittered in the late morning light. Ice covered its surface, creating a fractal barrier over its glass-like face. Peter stood at the lake's edge, a bone-deep weariness clinging to his shoulders. A constant tension had worked its way into his limbs over the last month. It wasn't just the heavy workload that came with restoring a fractured town like DeVerre. Nor was it the rigorous exercise routine the Warden had implemented to train them to ensure Cassandra's protection.

This weariness was heavier than mental or physical fatigue. It was an exhaustion of the soul. One that crept across his skin like the frost that encased the lake.

Blowing out a puff of air that turned into a brilliant fog in front of his face, Peter shoved the anxiety out of his body. Two and a half months ago, he and his brother, Spencer, had moved to DeVerre. In that time, Peter had nearly died too many times to count—he'd almost lost Spencer a half a dozen different ways as well. He had helped uncover and destroy a cult, been taken prisoner and tortured by a beast of the spirit world, and watched one of his best friends die.

Peter's thumb flicked the band of the gold ring on his right ring finger. He supposed anxiety was a natural reaction to so many haunting experiences.

Snow drifted slowly around him, flecking his shoulders and head with the white powder. The forest was frozen in the Washingtonian winter. Everything was white around him, only small glimpses of the pines and underbrush peeking through to veriegate the scenery.

Peter had been taking daily walks through the woods and to the lake over the past month. Although his nightmares had vanished with the valravn, he couldn't shake the tightening feeling of claustrophobia when he spent too long indoors. He started walking in the woods to clear his mind, knowing the practice always worked for Spencer. The fresh air and wide winter sky offered a welcome reprieve after his time in Alexander Frossard's vault cell.

Over time, Peter found himself making the long trek to DeVerre Lake, searching the shoreline for ghosts.

The faded spirits of deceased Wielders lingering around the lake drifted among the trees—men and women from centuries ago. Since he started these walks to the lake, he'd helped several ghosts find peace, including Mike Mercier's grandfather, Clarence. When he explained that he and his brother, as Varons, had expelled the Druids from DeVerre, Clarence let out a relieved sob and said, "Then I can rest, knowing I didn't fail them."

Peter wasn't entirely sure what the man meant, but he didn't get a chance to ask as Clarence's gray form dissipated. A tingle had raced along Peter's spine that had nothing to do with the winter wind, and he'd heard a whisper echo around him—a sound beyond sound—just before the ghost swirled away into nothingness, leaving behind a permeating sense of peace.

For the first time, Peter understood why Cassandra had been so impacted by her experience with that ghost, Katherine, when she was a girl. Helping ghosts find peace was addictive. It soaked into your spirit, giving it unexplainable hope and joy. And Peter needed some joy right about now.

Still, helping other ghosts find peace wasn't why Peter came to the lake every day. He was looking for Anna.

Yesterday marked one month since her death. Peter and Connor had spent nearly all their free time searching for information on how to resurrect Anna. With the Varon and Frossard vaults at his fingertips, Peter was confident there would be something that could give them answers. And while he and Connor had found some additional references and clues, it wasn't enough. Nor did it matter when the most critical step was finding the ghost of the person you intended to resurrect.

As Anna's ghost had yet to appear at all, Peter was beginning to question if their research even mattered. He'd been skeptical of her becoming a ghost in the first place. There was a good chance she'd chosen to move on and find peace all on her own.

Connor insisted she hadn't. He believed she'd become a ghost because it wasn't her time to die. Of course, that could be his denial and desperation to get back the woman he loved.

To make matters worse, neither Peter nor Connor had enough time to research. While Connor was in Spokane finishing his final year of medical school, Peter was busy helping set DeVerre to rights. They'd lost a considerable number of their populace to the Druids, only to gain a large influx of residents in the Warden members sent to rebuild the town. And as the newly named "true Varon," people began to look to Peter for guidance.

Silas Varon, their distant cousin who'd helped them reclaim DeVerre from the Druids, had returned to his home in Gold Mountain for the holiday season. While his request for a transfer to DeVerre to help with the transition had been approved, the Warden required him to return to Gold Mountain until his replacement could be sent. As it was

Thanksgiving and now Christmas, they'd pushed his family's move back to the beginning of the year.

That left Peter, Spencer, and their friends to figure everything out on their own. They had to navigate the politics, all while proving their ability to protect Cassandra as the new Vessel for the Spectral, which the Druids had released a month ago. Though the Spectral hadn't shown up yet, that didn't make Cassandra any safer. Her life was marked now, making her a "collectible" that the Druids would do anything to obtain.

Their lives had changed completely. Now, Peter, Spencer, and Cassandra all had personal trainers and nutritionists working hard to get them into top shape so they could withstand any strain their bodies might face. They were also required to undergo intense Wielder training to improve their connections to the spirit world. If the Druids came, they needed to be able to protect Cassandra without question.

Beyond that, there was now a fifty-person detail assigned to watch over Cassandra at all times. Usually, they accomplished this by sitting in a car on the grounds of Occasus or following her around town. Though according to the Warden reps, they were far more lax with Cassandra's detail than other Vessels', knowing that Peter and Spencer were at her side, day and night.

Still, all of the changes were beginning to agitate Peter.

With a final sigh, he turned away from the lake. There had been no sign of Anna, only a few ghosts drifting around the forest in the early afternoon. He had taken his walk after their training session that morning. Though his body initially struggled with the rigorous training, he was starting to build the endurance needed. The daily walks probably contributed to that, even though he went to bed almost every night feeling like he'd been hit by a truck.

Walking back through the Blackwood Forest toward Occasus, Peter slipped his frigid hands into his coat pockets. Christmas was five days away, and it felt like any other week filled with training, Warden meetings, and Spectral prep. They'd be lucky to celebrate the holiday at all.

Their mom had been disappointed when they'd told her they couldn't make it back to Norfolk for Christmas. Thankfully, she hadn't suggested coming to DeVerre, since they'd already made plans to visit with the aging parents of their stepdad, Ben. Peter didn't know what they'd have done if she'd asked. She still didn't know anything about the spirit world, and Christmas didn't seem the time to introduce her to it.

But as this would be their first Christmas without their mom around, it hardly felt like a holiday at all.

Crunching through the wintry forest, Peter set his jaw. He'd had it with this heaviness and anxiety. It was Christmastime, and he wouldn't let the holiday go by without a proper celebration.

After his long hike, Peter slipped through the back gate and onto Occasus's large, snow-covered, and pine-dotted property. The grand mansion stood like a memorial in the middle of the forest, commemorating the Varons who gave their lives to defend the Veil of DeVerre. Its multi-tiered roof was blanketed in white. A drift of gray-tinged smoke puffed out of the chimney.

Peter's heart lifted every time he saw their home. How you could become so attached to a house in such a short time would never cease to baffle him. But after not quite three months, he could never imagine living anywhere but Occasus for the rest of his life.

Mounting the short staircase onto the wraparound porch, Peter entered through the back door. The empty kitchen greeted him with the still lingering scent of coffee. Though he'd left more than two hours before, neither Spencer nor Cassandra had had lunch yet, it seemed. Peter rolled his eyes. He felt like their mother sometimes, having to remind them both to eat.

Unzipping his coat and removing his beanie, Peter moved into the house. He found Spencer typing away on his laptop in the office while Cassandra lounged opposite him in one of the two chairs they'd purchased since she and Peter did so much work in there with him these days. Anguis and Nex sprawled on the rug, the fireplace crackling behind them. Peter recognized the book in Cassandra's hands as the one that Jeremiah Rhader—head of the Warden's task force sent to DeVerre for the protection of the Vessel—gave her to learn more about Spectrals.

"What are you two doing?" Peter asked, resolved in his newly created plan.

Spencer barely glanced up at him, still typing as he said, "Hang on."

Cassandra spun a highlighter between her fingers, eyes on her book. "Working," she said.

"Well, stop," Peter instructed.

"I'm in the middle of a scene, Pete," Spencer said distractedly.

That caused him to pause. "For *Wenzel & Frankly?*"

"Yeah." Spencer typed another few words before his bright eyes lifted from the laptop screen. "I'll have the Christmas special revisions ready for your approval by the end of the day."

"Oh, cool." Peter shrugged off his coat. He draped it over the back of his chair—a brown leather wing chair with a low, tufted back that looked like it belonged in a *Sherlock Holmes* film. "Did you see my notes from last night?"

"What do you think I was working on?"

Peter smirked. "It was a good idea, wasn't it?"

Spencer gave him a bland look. "Just because I have a girlfriend now doesn't mean I suddenly like writing romance," he said.

"You're the one who created Serene," Peter reminded him. "It's not my fault that Frankly finds her irresistible."

Cassandra snorted, tapping her highlighter against her page.

"Anyway," Peter brushed his hand through the air, refusing to be deterred from his idea, "wrap that up ASAP, okay? We're on Christmas break, starting now. Or," he paused, motioning to the laptop, "starting as soon as you're done with the edit."

"You have to read and approve it when I'm done," Spencer said.

Peter huffed long-sufferingly. "Fine. Once you've completed your edit and I've approved it, we're on Christmas break." He reached down and shut Cassandra's book. "That means you, too, kid."

"Hey!" Cassandra slapped his hand. "I was in the middle of a sentence."

"So, you weren't listening to a word I was saying?"

She shrugged. "Sometimes you ramble, and I find it's more efficient to keep working."

Peter gave her a disapproving frown. "Whatever. Get your last bits of work in because that's it for the rest of the week. It's Christmas, and it's time to celebrate. We're gonna make Reubens, watch movies, keep *If On A Winter's Night* on freakin' repeat, and eat a mountain of cookies."

Cassandra raised her hand. "What do Reubens have to do with Christmas?"

"It's our traditional Christmas meal," Spencer explained. "Mom got tired of ham."

"And what's that *Winter's Night* thing?"

"Sting's Christmas album." Spencer sighed then, leaning on the desk. "Pete, it's a nice idea, but none of us really feel like celebrating."

"That's the point!" Peter insisted. "No one feels like it, so we've *got* to. It's Christmas. The time for peace. And this town could seriously use some peace."

Spencer and Cassandra shared a look.

"We all could," Peter added.

They knew it was true. After a month of sorrow, rebuilding, struggling, working, researching, and adapting to their new reality, they could use the joy and rest that the Christmas season brought.

A small smile worked its way onto Spencer's face. "All right," he said. "I'm in."

"Me too," Cassandra agreed.

"What's first on the agenda?" Spencer asked.

Peter opened his mouth, then realized he didn't know the answer. He pulled his notebook out of his coat pocket. "Let's make a list. All the things I've already mentioned, of course. But what were all the holiday traditions Mom used to force on us as kids?"

"Too many to count," Spencer said.

"Maybe I should call her," Peter mused.

"That's not a bad idea. We haven't talked to her in a few weeks."

"And it is Christmas," Cassandra pointed out.

"Yeah, exactly." Peter snapped his fingers decisively. "I'll give her a call, and you guys brainstorm what you can think of. Then we'll reconvene and make our plans."

Spencer tapped the desktop. "Doesn't Connor get back today? We can ask for his input too."

"Good thinking." Peter exchanged his notebook for his phone. "I should probably also let Rhader know we'll be taking the rest of the week off. A regimented nutrition plan and Christmas cookies aren't typically friends."

"We should still work out, though," Spencer said.

Peter waved his hand. "Fine, whatever. Exercise is acceptable, but that's the extent of it. If anyone needs anything in the next week, they'll just have to wait. True Varon's orders."

Cassandra grinned wryly, and Spencer shook his head, but neither of them objected.

Scooping his coat off the chair, Peter headed for the front closet. He dialed Rhader's number and tucked the phone under his ear as he put the coat away. The Warden agent answered quickly, his deep voice rumbling through the line. "Mr. Varon," he said by way of greeting.

"Hey, Rhader." Peter hurried up the stairs, taking them two at a time, then regretted it as his breath caught. His conditioning still wasn't what he wanted it to be. He cleared his throat, then gave the man his plans.

Jeremiah Rhader was a no-nonsense, direct sort of person. Tall, dark-skinned, and somewhere in his late fifties, the man was impressively well-built, and Peter was convinced he could intimidate a grizzly bear. His rich brown eyes had this way of threatening with a single look. In the past month of knowing the man, Peter hadn't seen him crack a smile once.

Needless to say, it was Peter's new life goal to annoy the man until he finally broke that impossibly stoic demeanor.

"So, what'd'ya think, Rhader?" he asked cheerily. "Give us the week off?"

There was a long pause on the other end of the phone. Peter could imagine the man brushing his long fingers over his immaculately trimmed black beard. "Very well," Rhader said at last. "But I have some conditions."

Rhader listed his demands: first, they had to attend the town events throughout the week—the tree lighting in the plaza that night and the Christmas Eve service. Then, any work delayed by their holiday was to be handled first thing on Monday, December 27. Finally, their detail would remain on duty the whole time, ensuring Cassandra's safety.

Finding the stipulations acceptable, Peter got off the phone with Rhader and called his mom.

Mallory Collins-Powell answered with an excited, "Merry Christmas, Petey! What are you up to? Is it snowing there?"

Used to his mom's flurry of questions, Peter smiled as he took a seat on his bed. "Mom, when isn't it snowing here?" he replied.

"I'm jealous!" Mallory sighed dreamily. "The news says we're getting a cold front, but no snow."

"You'll just have to join us next Christmas."

"Ben and I are already looking at tickets. Do you have a guest room?"

Peter glanced toward the back of the house where the spare was located. They'd given it to Connor for when he wasn't at medical school, but he'd be moved out by next Christmas.

"Yeah," Peter confirmed. "It's kind of small, but maybe Spence and Cass will be married by then, and you can have his old room."

"Ooh," Mallory crooned with interest. "Do you think they're that serious? They've only been together a month, right?"

"Well, yeah, but have you ever known Spencer to date a girl? At all?"

Mallory chuckled. "He's taken girls on dates."

"Like, twice."

"You have a point. Now, did you call to talk about your brother's love life, or did you need something, Petey?"

Slipping out his notebook again, Peter put the phone on speaker. "Actually, yeah. We're making a list of must-do Christmas activities, and I wanted to make sure we didn't forget anything."

"You called the right person," Mallory said excitedly. Then, for the next fifteen minutes, she chronicled every last Christmas event they'd ever done.

Peter soaked up the joy in Mallory's voice. If he couldn't spend Christmas day with his mom, then at least he could do all the traditions that would make her feel right there with them. And maybe then he could thaw the frost that clung to his heart.

CHAPTER TWO

Cassandra

As Peter's boots pounded up the stairs, Cassandra turned back to Spencer, the book on Spectrals lying closed on her lap. "Well," she said with amusement, "it seems like Peter's finally back to his old self."

Spencer stared at the hall, massaging his palm. A heavy knowing lingered in his glazed-over eyes. "No," he said softly. "This is a distraction. He's still hiding something."

Cassandra raised her brow. "Hiding something?"

With a shake of his head, Spencer turned back to her. "Never mind. Pete's just trying to get through this."

She sighed, feeling the weight of the past month as though it were an entire library settled on her shoulders. "We all are," she said.

"Which," Spencer gave her a small smile, "is why we agreed to this scheme of his."

Cassandra returned his grin, knowing it was true. Over the past month, they'd struggled to break out of the pain and stress of their new lives. She was still coming to terms with the fact that she was a Vessel, now a host for a spirit-being of unknown power and purpose. They'd been training hard, learning all they could while also helping rebuild DeVerre. She and Spencer had found moments of happiness together, enjoying their new relationship. While they'd tried to help Peter, he was dealing with more than either of them could quite understand, having returned from capture and torture, losing Anna, and becoming the true Varon.

And that was part of the reason Cassandra had insisted that the brothers get back to their work as authors. Not only did they need time together, just the two of them, but they also needed to achieve their dreams. She wouldn't let them sacrifice everything for her, no matter how willing they said they were.

"You moved to DeVerre to get your career off the ground," she'd told them weeks ago. *"You can't let that go because things have gotten hard."*

Though she'd had to push, the brothers had given in without too much of a fight. Now, they were finishing up a Christmas special that would announce their temporary break from the serial publication of *Wenzel & Frankly* to complete the first book in the official series.

Spencer shut his laptop. "So," he began, "Christmas activities. Whatcha got?"

At his teasing tone, she set her book on the desk. "Obviously, decorating the tree."

"Obviously," he mimicked.

"Though we'll have to get one first."

"Consider it on the list."

"Then, we'll have to have a snowball fight."

"Of course."

"And make snow angels."

"Iconic."

Cassandra lounged in her chair, enjoying the way his blue eyes twinkled at her. "And then, there's always the classic movies and popcorn."

Spencer leaned on the desk, engaged in the conversation. "I bet you're a *Wonderful Life* kind of a girl."

"Actually," Cassandra raised a teasing brow, "I find it boring."

He laughed softly in that warm way that made her feel like she'd been wrapped in a quilt. "Then what are your favorites?"

"I'm partial to *Just Friends*," she said. "And *Home Alone*—the second one in particular, where they're in New York. Though *While You Were Sleeping* is a classic, and I watch it every year."

"I didn't peg you as a Christmas comedy fan."

She waved a hand through the air. "Classic Christmas movies are too sappy. But you're definitely a *White Christmas* and *Miracle on 34th Street* boy."

He grinned slyly. "I prefer *Die Hard*."

"Seriously?" Cassandra scrunched her nose in disbelief. "I always forget that's a Christmas movie."

"Yeah, once Mom let us watch it when we were teens, Pete made it a whole deal. We watch it every year while wrapping gifts. It's silly, but it stuck. We can quote the whole thing at this point."

She frowned playfully. "Then, we can't watch it together."

"Why not?"

"If we're wrapping presents, we can't be in the same room. And you're not getting a sneak peek at your gift."

Spencer's smile grew softer. "You got me a gift?"

"I'd be a crappy girlfriend if I didn't."

"You couldn't be a crappy girlfriend if you tried." He sat back contentedly. "I got you a gift too."

"Good," she said lightly. "I'd hate to have to break up with you so soon."

He chuckled just as Cassandra's phone started ringing. Her eyes drifted down to where it sat on the desk. She frowned at the caller ID. "It's my dad," she said.

When she made no move to answer, Spencer asked, "Don't you think you should talk to him?"

"Not really."

"He's your dad, Cass." Spencer's voice was gentle but pressing. "And it's Christmas."

Cassandra looked up at him, catching the adamance in his stare. A month ago, she'd chosen to leave her family behind. She was no longer a Clement in her mind. While she didn't know what that made her—an orphan by choice, maybe?—she wasn't willing to return to the toxicity of her childhood. She wanted to move forward as a part of a new family, Peter and Spencer's family.

But Spencer wouldn't understand that. He came from a loving, supportive home with parents and a brother who would quite literally die for one another. Even if she tried to explain, he'd say that she should give them another chance.

With a sigh, Cassandra picked up her phone. "I'll be back," she muttered, walking out of the office. Knowing that the call would end if she didn't answer soon, she pressed the green button on the screen while she moved through the dining room. "Hello?"

"Hi, sweetheart," Allen Clement said, his voice gentle on the other side. "Merry Christmas."

Cassandra returned the holiday salutation as she stepped up to the large picture window. She watched the snowfall as she listened to her dad speak. "I know you're probably busy, so I won't keep you long," he was saying, "but your mother and I wanted to invite you to Christmas dinner. We . . . we don't like how we left things, and we want to make it right. As it's the season for that kind of thing, we were hoping you'd come so that we could apologize and show you that we mean to be better."

Cassandra played with the lace curtains, unsure what to say. She should say no. Shouldn't she? She'd decided against them. But as she tried to form the word, it felt wrong on her tongue. "I'll have to think about it, Dad."

"We completely understand," he said with almost too much good-heartedness. "If you do choose to come, just know, you're welcome to bring Spencer too. And his brother, if he'd like to join."

Surprised that he remembered Spencer's name, Cassandra nodded, though he couldn't see it. She'd only mentioned Spencer once, in passing. In the past, her parents would have intentionally forgotten a detail like that to belittle her time in DeVerre.

In her confusion, she found herself saying, "All right. I'll let you know."

"Wonderful. I look forward to hearing from you," he said, then added, "Love you."

Cassandra bit out the affectation before ending the call in a rush. She stared at the screen for a lingering second. Why hadn't she said no? She could face a horde of beasts and a cult of Druids, but she couldn't tell her parents "no"?

Shoving her disappointment down, Cassandra returned to the office. She dropped her phone back onto the desk and sat across from Spencer once more. "Sorry," she said. "Where were we?"

"You, not breaking up with me," Spencer said distractedly. He nodded toward her phone. "What'd he want?"

"Oh, he just—" Cassandra brushed her hand through the air flippantly. "My parents want us to come for Christmas."

"Oh. What did you tell him?"

"I said I'd think about it." She shook her head. "But I should have just said no. I'm not putting either of us through that. And now," she sighed, "I either have to call him back and explain myself, or text and look like a jerk."

Spencer picked at the edge of the desk. "Or," he said cautiously, "we could go."

She sent him a look of immediate shock.

He held up a placating hand. "Just—hear me out, okay? You said they want *us* to come. That means they invited me, right?"

"Yeah," she confirmed. "You *and* Peter, actually."

"Okay," he said, his tone almost hopeful. "So, wouldn't that make things better? Even if your parents try to guilt you into staying, Pete and

I will be there. And if they invited us, it sounds like they're acting far more understanding already. Why wouldn't we go?"

"Why *would* we?" Cassandra countered. "Spence, my parents lied to me for my entire life. I'm not willing to put myself in that kind of situation again."

He pursed his lips, but she kept going. "I already decided," she said determinedly. "I'm done with Spokane and with them. I'm not a Clement anymore, no matter what my name says."

"Cass," he said softly, "they're your family."

She tensed at his tender gaze, but his next words broke her resolve.

"I think I should meet them at least once."

Cassandra sighed. "Spencer, you don't have to."

"I want to."

"Why?"

"Because they're a part of you," he said. "Whether you like it or not."

Cassandra had no argument against that. What could she say? Just like she'd expected, Spencer didn't understand. Worse, he had a point. He and his annoying logic could very well convince her to give up her resolve and go to Spokane so he could meet her parents and better understand her. Which, she supposed, might be the best outcome. Maybe then he'd see just how bad it was.

Peter showed up then, his notebook ready in his hand. "All right, I've got a whole list," he said, cheerfully oblivious to the tension in the room. "Mom says hi, by the way. And she wants to do a video call on Christmas."

Spencer turned to him. "How would you feel about going to Spokane for a day or two?" he asked.

Peter stalled, his brow furrowing. "Uh ... For like, shopping or something?"

"Cass's parents want the three of us to come for Christmas."

He took his seat. "Like, Christmas Day?"

Spencer turned to Cassandra for clarification.

"He didn't say," she replied. "Maybe."

Spencer pursed his lips in thought. "I think we should spend Christmas Day at Occasus," he said. "But maybe we could go for Christmas Eve."

"Or Christmas Eve eve," Peter suggested. "Rhader said it's fine for us to take the next few days off, but he strongly suggested we make a showing at the Christmas Eve service."

"All right, so how's this?" Spencer held out his hand as though physically offering his plan. "We go to your parents' on the twenty-third, have dinner or whatever, and that'll be it? Then, I can meet them, but it's not a huge commitment or anything."

Cassandra didn't want to give in. She wanted to cut off her family and never think about them again. But Spencer was right. They were a part of her life. They were a part of *her*—the girl she'd once been and the woman she'd become. Even if she never had a relationship with them again, it would be good for him to understand.

"Okay," Cassandra agreed. "I'll call my dad tomorrow and let him know. But for now, let's hear what you've got, Peter."

"Great!" Peter held his notebook open. "First, we've gotta get a tree."

"We had the same thought," Spencer said.

Peter put a check mark on the page. "Which, of course, will include decorating it. Mom reminded me that we need to make ornaments and a garland."

Cassandra tipped her brow up in surprise. "You make your own ornaments?"

"Just one each year," Spencer said. "It was a fun craft as a kid, and Mom loves that kind of stuff, so we just kept doing it."

She smirked. "What? Do you make popsicle stick trees or something?"

"Trees, reindeer, snowmen, houses," Peter listed, then shrugged. "The works."

While Cassandra sniggered at the idea of grown men decorating popsicle sticks, Spencer gave her an annoyed look. "We *used* to do that," he said. "Over the years, we branched into clay, leather, wood, and felt. We got pretty good at it."

"That sounds adorable," Cassandra said, completely genuine.

Spencer gave her a dry grin before turning back to Peter. "Even if all four of us make an ornament," he said, including Connor in their plans, "we'll need more for the tree."

"Diane has decorations in the attic," Cassandra offered. "Like, boxes and boxes of decorations. She was a huge fan of Christmas."

"Perfect," Peter exclaimed. "We'll get those down as soon as we finish our list."

He made a note, then looked up at them. "It's too late to get the tree today, so we'll do that tomorrow. Next on the agenda: cookies."

"We could do that tomorrow afternoon," Spencer suggested. "After we decorate the tree."

Not one for baking, Cassandra pursed her lips. "We don't have the stuff for cookie making."

Peter brushed the problem off. "I'll go shopping for all that this evening." He tapped the notebook page. "We also need stuff for the Reubens, and Mom gave me the recipe for her gingerbread French toast for Christmas morning."

"Oh, yeah!" Spencer nodded vehemently. "We *have* to have that."

Amused by their enthusiasm for all things holiday, Cassandra smiled. "You guys had really elaborate Christmases, didn't you?"

The brothers shared a bemused look, as though their list wasn't growing egregiously long.

"I mean, kind of," Spencer said. "We went all out on the traditions and things, but gift-giving wasn't as big a deal. Our friends would always talk about getting dozens of presents each year, but our parents always kept it pretty small. It might've been a money thing—"

"Not really," Peter interrupted. "I mean, yeah, things were tight since Mom stayed home and stuff, but I heard them talking, and it was a choice. They didn't want us thinking that Christmas was about getting stuff."

Spencer shrugged, accepting the answer readily. "Sounds like something Dad would say."

Cassandra liked seeing this side of the brothers. While it wasn't exactly rare for them to talk about their parents, it was unusual for her to get such details of their lives as children. Even if she could never be part of their past, these conversations made her feel like she was anyway. And since she would never get to know David Collins, these memories were her one opportunity.

"I'll be sure not to expect much then," Cassandra said lightheartedly.

Peter and Spencer turned to her with amused expressions.

"Oh, we give great gifts," Peter said happily. "There might only be one or two, but they're always quality."

"Mm." Cassandra leaned back in her seat. "Prepare to be disappointed in my gifts then. I'm not known for my gifting skills."

Peter smirked. "It's the thought that counts, right? Besides, you're the one who came up with Connor's gift idea, and that was a home run."

"That's left to be seen," Cassandra said. "Are *Die Hard* and gift wrapping on your list?"

Peter glanced at Spencer, who said, "We talked about it."

With a nod, Peter gestured toward his notebook. "It's number three," he said. "Any other Christmas movies we have to watch?"

They tossed a handful of titles around, including many that Cassandra and Spencer had previously mentioned. They wound up with a list too long to watch alongside all the other activities on their list. When they tried to find time to schedule it all, they had to cut most of them. After all, if they were going to visit Spokane, that would take up an entire evening.

Once they narrowed down the list, Peter reminded them of the Christmas tree lighting in the plaza that night. "Owen told me they typically do it earlier in the season," he said. "But with everything, they decided to postpone it."

"With how busy we've been," Spencer said, "I can only imagine how slammed Owen and Tom are, trying to keep a grip on the town while helping the Warden settle in."

"I'm just glad they're lighting the tree at all," Cassandra added, reaching down to scratch the top of Anguis's head. "Diane and I always went together, so it'll be good to keep the tradition alive."

"Speaking of Diane—" Peter pointed to the ceiling. "You guys ready to dive into a mountain of dust to get those decorations?"

"It's not that bad," Cassandra replied.

Peter gave her a flat look. "Last time we searched around up there, we were sneezing for a week straight."

"It's an attic," Spencer said, standing. "What do you expect?"

Following him, Cassandra and Peter rose from their seats. The dogs jumped up too. And together, they wound their way to the top of Occasus to dig the Christmas decorations out of the back corner of the attic where Cassandra and Diane had placed them last year.

Hefting one of the several boxes, Cassandra couldn't help but smile as she thought about the memories she'd created with Diane Larkin over the past four years and imagined the new ones she'd make with the Varon brothers now. Whether or not it was a distraction, she was grateful for this idea of Peter's. After everything they'd faced, they did need the peace and joy that only the Christmas season could bring. And she looked forward to every moment she got to spend celebrating with the Collins brothers.

CHAPTER THREE

Connor

The aged welcome sign of DeVerre was covered in snow. Only bits of the wood showed through, revealing the smallest snippet of the emerald-green painted town slogan.

Connor tightened his jaw, glad he didn't have to look at the updated sign. A couple of weeks ago, Peter had informed him that the new town council had agreed to remove the population count from the sign and simplify the slogan to *"Where the pines grow tall"* to make the place feel friendlier.

Though Connor understood the desire to leave behind the old DeVerre—the one filled with murder, secrets, and Druids—he couldn't help feeling it was a betrayal to the hometown he loved. No matter how screwed up the place might have been, it was his home. It was Anna's home. And he didn't like the Warden coming in, changing it all.

The two-lane road broke through the thick trees, leading Connor back into the town. Under the overcast sky, the landscape was tinged in a dull white and silvery gray. The grass, the trees, the buildings—everything was blanketed in snow. It felt ominous and weighty. It was as though the world was just as worn out and cold as his heart.

One month.

It had been one whole month since he'd lost Anna. Since he'd watch that wendigo snap her neck.

And he still didn't know how to save her.

Shortly after the Final Unleashing and the eradication of the Druids, Connor had to return to Spokane to continue medical school. While becoming a doctor was as expected of him as becoming the Elder of the Druidic Faction in DeVerre, he actually *wanted* to be a doctor. And now that his father was dead—now that Connor had committed patricide—the town needed a new doctor. So no matter how much it felt like a waste of time to sit in class and take exams, he worked hard, determined to graduate so that he could come home and become the man he'd wished he could be—the man Anna believed he was, the man she'd loved.

A muscle in Connor's jaw twitched.

He was determined not only to become that man, but also to give her that life of which she'd always dreamed. Of course, they had to find Anna's ghost first. And then they had to figure out how to bring her back, which was looking more impossible each day.

Through all his schooling over the last month, Connor had taken every opportunity he could to research resurrection. With Peter's help, he'd made slow progress. It wasn't as though Connor could contact his old Druid friends (not that he had many, to begin with), and they'd all decided it best not to inform the Warden of Anna's death from the outset. Silas and Owen had informed them that resurrection was a touchy subject, some believing the dead should stay dead, while others thought it was sacrilegious even to suggest such a thing was possible outside of Christ's influence. As only the Varon brothers, Cassandra, the Lamberts, Silas, Haley's brothers, Gabe, and Juliet Chapelle knew of Anna's death, they'd told the rest of the town that Anna had gone to Canada to live with her parents and grandparents as she recovered from the trauma of being a hostage.

Even if they had chosen to talk about her resurrection to the Warden, Connor doubted they'd trust him with that sort of information. He was still an ex-Druid, which was as good as saying that he was a double agent in the Warden's eyes. Which Connor couldn't fault them for. After what happened in Porthaven . . .

Connor had spoken with Jeremiah Rhader, the head of the Warden within DeVerre, to offer all the information he had on the Druids. It wasn't as much as he would have liked; his dad had been withholding over the years, likely due to Connor's concerning relationship with the Lamberts. It seemed that Alexander always suspected his son's disloyalty.

And even though Rhader had readily accepted his knowledge, Connor wasn't comfortable sharing his plans with the man. The Warden wasn't known for their openness, and there was a chance they'd try to stop Peter and Connor in their resurrection of Anna should they catch wind of it. When Connor had explained his reservations to Peter, he'd agreed readily. They talked to Ava and Owen, and from there, the choice was made.

Turning off the main road, Connor pulled into the parking lot of the gas station and mechanic shop. He saw Aaron's motorcycle resting on the side of the building, and he pulled to a stop beside it. They'd renewed their friendship over the last month, talking almost as much as Connor had with Peter. Though Aaron was only a Herald Wielder, able to see ghosts but not interact with them, he was just as determined to bring back Anna as Connor and Peter. In truth, all the Lamberts were—including Owen and Haley. And that made Connor sure of their success.

Even if Anna's ghost was still missing.

Connor unbuckled his seatbelt and turned off the car. He clenched his keys in his hand, letting their jagged edges bite into his palm as he climbed out of the Land Rover. Anna was still out there. He knew that. Maybe she wouldn't hold on to life of her own accord, but she wasn't gone for good. She had to be out there. Because it wasn't her time.

Connor looked up at the snowy gray sky and muttered an internal prayer, *"Please. Don't take her yet."*

He'd found himself praying regularly over the last month. Mostly in anger. But he knew that Anna would be proud of him, telling him that it's better to yell at God than to ignore Him. So, Connor had started sending every complaint and hope up to the Heavens.

That was the thing about being raised as a Druid; Connor knew there was a spirit world. He knew there was a higher power. Even though the Druids believed that to be Gaia, or Mother Nature, as most people called her, Connor had gone to DeVerre Chapel his entire life with Anna at his side. And he'd seen the truth in the way she and her family lived.

There was a divine power. And Connor knew He didn't live in the earth beneath their feet but in the spirit of every person who invited Him into their lives. Connor had to believe that because how could people like Owen Bernard and Silas Varon—men who were good, strong, loving, and dedicated, what real men should be—how could they be wrong?

And now that Connor had met the Warden himself, he was even more convinced they *were* the good guys . . . even if they did have some questionable policies.

Connor stepped inside Durand's Mechanic Garage, his face flushed from the transition of the car's heater to the frigid wind to the shop's heat. He shivered, scanning the garage. He spotted Aaron in the far corner, working on an old Subaru.

Aaron pushed the bridge of his glasses up his nose with the back of his hand, catching sight of Connor. "Oh, hey," Aaron said, a lilt of surprise in his tone. "Didn't realize you were getting back today."

"Yeah, I had my last exam this morning, so I left right after," Connor said. He leaned against the giant arm of the car lift that Aaron worked by. "Just wanted to stop by before heading to Occasus. Thought you'd like to know I found a lead last night."

"You finally found something, huh? Where?"

"One of the books I took from Dad's vault," Connor said. He and Peter had spent his last break emptying the Frossard vault, transferring the contents to Occasus. But Connor made sure to grab the three books that looked most promising before heading back to Spokane.

After weeks of dedicated reading, he'd found the first speck of information. He'd called Peter immediately, but he didn't think it was the sort of news to share with the Lamberts over the phone, especially when it was so minimal.

Connor crossed his arms, steeling himself for a dozen questions that he couldn't answer. "Sounds like resurrection often requires a sacrifice of some kind. Not sure what yet, though."

Aaron's brow furrowed as he stepped away from the Subaru. "A sacrifice, huh? On whose part?"

"The resurrector's," Connor said, knowing he'd be happy to pay whatever price Anna's life cost—even if that were his own.

Aaron seemed to know it too. "This was in a Druid book?"

"Yeah."

"Can we trust it?"

"As much as we can trust that they know what they're talking about," Connor said. "It was written by Druids, for Druids. As screwed up as they are, they wouldn't intentionally mislead one another. And they didn't foresee this book getting into Warden hands."

"Are we Warden?" Aaron asked casually.

Connor raised his brow.

Aaron shrugged. "Not saying I'm against them. Just saying, I'm not sure I'm with them."

"Trust me, Aaron. It's better to be with the Warden. I've seen what's on the other side, and no matter what secrets and issues these people have . . ." Connor pressed his lips together in a humorless smile. "Let's just say they have more honor than the Druids."

"Hm." Aaron stepped over to the workbench beside the lift. He picked up a rag and wiped off his grease-stained hands. "Well, thanks for letting me know," he said, then paused. His dark eyes flicked up to Connor. "I, uh—I think you should probably know: my parents will be in town for Christmas. We'll be telling people that Anna wasn't ready to come back, so she's staying to help with our grandparents."

Connor blanched. Andrew and Aimee Lambert had been like second parents to him growing up. He'd adored the couple. Then, he'd broken their daughter's heart, moved to Spokane, and hadn't seen them since. And now, he'd gotten Anna killed.

As much as he loved them, Connor had no doubt they'd never want to see him again.

"Oh, nice," Connor managed to say. He cleared his throat. "Should I, uh—would it be best if I stayed scarce? I mean, I don't want to ruin their Christmas, but . . ."

Aaron watched him steadily. The Lambert son was never one to press people. It's part of what made him such a good friend in Connor's mind. He patiently waited for Connor to work out his words in his head.

Connor finally concluded, "I'd like to apologize to them. I want them to know how sorry I am. For everything. And that I'm going to fix it." He paused, then added, "If you think that'd be okay. I'm assuming you've told them about the spirit world at this point."

"Mom already knew more or less," Aaron said somewhat bitterly. "But yeah, we caught them up on everything that's happened. And they'd like to talk with you too. Though I think they're a little more interested in meeting Peter and Spencer, to be honest, as the ones who started this whole thing in the first place."

Connor supposed it made sense, though he felt he was the one with more explaining to do.

"They'll be getting in tomorrow evening," Aaron continued. "So, maybe mention the idea of meeting up for dinner or something when you get back to Occasus."

"Will do." Connor straightened, taking a cautious step back from the lift. "See you around."

Aaron lifted a hand in farewell, and Connor took his leave of the garage. His chest constricted as he pushed out of the building. The cold air burned his lungs.

Andrew and Aimee were returning to DeVerre.

They'd moved to Canada a few years back to take care of Andrew's parents near Port McNeill. The Grandparents Lambert lived in a rural home, and, with their failing health, Andrew felt the urge to help them get into a more stable living situation. Last Connor heard, they'd begun the moving process, but Anna's grandfather, Roger, was a man of routine. Roger Lambert didn't want to leave his lifelong home, filled to the brim with memories and mementos. So, the process was taking longer than they'd hoped.

Back in his car, Connor wondered who was really taking care of Anna's grandparents while her parents were headed for DeVerre. This was the first Christmas they'd returned since their move. He knew Andrew had a sister, Hannah. But she was a big executive in Vancouver with a family of her own. Had the Lamberts had to hire someone?

With his father's estate still in probate and his mother missing, Connor didn't have much to his name. But he wondered if the Lamberts would let him pay for the care anyway.

Winding down the road, Connor refused to glance over as he passed Haven Boulevard. The old Frossard mansion wasn't his home anymore, and he refused to give it any further place in his life. It too was part of his father's will, and though the spirit world recognized Connor as the vault's new owner, the law recognized Giana as the house's *legal* owner; otherwise, he would have sold the place already.

Through the snow-laden pines and spruces, Connor could see the faint outline of Occasus's gabled roofs and open gates. He couldn't say the Varon house felt like a home to him. It held too much contention in his heart, too many memories of how much his parents despised the Varon lineage and their nefarious plans to bring them down. It reminded him too much of the spirit world and its influence on his life.

But he couldn't deny the way his shoulders relaxed, knowing that inside those old walls were three people who wouldn't demand anything he couldn't give.

The Varon brothers and Cassandra Clement were surprisingly great people. After twenty-five years of living with cruel, calculating cult leaders, Connor found the unmitigated (sometimes overbearing) friendliness of Peter, the steady goodness of Spencer, and the absolute loyalty of Cassandra refreshing.

Connor drove past the sedan by the gate, holding two Warden members on detail to keep an eye on Cassandra. He parked next to the Jeep and truck in the drive, spotting the dogs running through the snowy lawn. They bounded over to him as he got out of his SUV, sniffing his pant legs. Connor wasn't used to pets, so he just said an uneasy, "hello, dogs," and kept his hands to himself as he headed up the porch steps.

Knowing the brothers kept the house locked, Connor pulled out his key. As he opened the door, he was surprised to hear laughter and heavy footsteps on the other side. Connor stepped into the entry hall to find Peter, Spencer, and Cassandra coming down the stairs, arms loaded with cardboard boxes.

"Hey!" Peter exclaimed upon seeing him. "Welcome home, man. Whoops! Wanna help us out?"

"What's going on?" Connor asked, moving to catch the small box Peter had almost dropped from the top of his stack.

"We're decorating," Cassandra announced, moving into the living room.

"For what?"

"For Christmas," Peter said, like that should be obvious.

"Why?" Even if Connor did care about the holiday, he wouldn't feel like celebrating this year. Not with Anna gone. It would be a monumental waste of time when they could be working on saving her.

"Look," Peter set his remaining boxes on the coffee table, "I get that there are a lot of reasons we *wouldn't* want to celebrate. But it's *Christmas*. And we need a break."

Connor unceremoniously dropped the small box on the couch. "Fine." He yanked the sleeves of his coat from his arms. "Take a break if you want. I'm gonna keep figuring out how to save Anna."

"It's not—" Peter sighed, Spencer and Cassandra sharing a look behind him. "I'm not saying that we'll stop searching for a way to save her. I'm just saying that it's been really heavy around here lately, and we could use some holiday cheer right about now. So, we're officially on break from Warden work, and we're gonna decorate for Christmas, eat a whole dozen cookies each, sing some carols, and get ourselves a tree."

Connor bristled, pausing as he hung up his coat. "You do realize that Christmas trees are a Druidic tradition, don't you?"

"Technically," Spencer cut in, "the tradition started in Germany where they set up trees in their houses and hung wafers on it to symbolize the eucharist—or communion, as it's more commonly known these days."

Cassandra gave Spencer a wry grin. "You're such a nerd."

He shrugged. "I had to look it up for the *Wenzel & Frankly* Christmas special."

"Whatever," Connor said, not wanting anything to do with his family's past. "You guys have fun, I guess."

"Hey, hey!" Peter stopped Connor from going up the stairs. "You have to participate in these holiday festivities too."

"Actually, I don't."

"As a resident of Occasus, you do." He grinned smugly. "Our house, our rules."

Seeing that he wouldn't budge, Connor scoffed. "I'll see if I can stay with Aaron while I'm in town."

"Wait, wait, wait—" Peter hurried forward, meeting him in the hall. His voice pitched lower, pleading. "Dude, you need this," he whispered. "You need time to chill, to recognize what the season is about."

Connor wasn't about to be moved.

Then Peter played the trump card. "It's what Anna would want."

Connor gritted his teeth. Somehow, in only a month and a half, Peter had come to understand Anna just as well as her siblings. It made him a great but obnoxious friend.

"Fine," Connor grumbled. "For Anna."

"Great!" Peter exclaimed. "Now, we've got the decorations down, but we need to make a shopping list for cookies, Christmas dinner, and stuff. Zeus," he said, pointing at Connor (who secretly liked the nickname but would never admit it even if someone put him in a cage with a valravn for a decade), "why don't you come with me to the store? Spence and Cass can get this place all decked out in the meantime."

Spencer and Cassandra nodded in agreement while Connor reluctantly accepted his role in the merrymaking.

Peter motioned toward the window, where the midday light left the world hazy and gray. "We don't have enough sunlight left to find a tree today, so we'll have to go cut it down tomorrow."

"Hang on," Spencer interjected. "You want to go out into the forest to *chop* a tree down?"

"Yeah," Peter said as though that were perfectly normal.

"I thought we'd just pick one up at a tree farm."

Cassandra gave Spencer an amused look. "Have you seen a tree farm in DeVerre?" she said.

"Well, no," he admitted. "I just figured the mill would cut them down and sell them there."

Peter brushed the idea off. "This is more fun anyway. In the shed out back, I found a saw, so we'll take that and pick out the biggest tree we can find."

Connor raised his brow, imagining Peter cutting down a towering pine. It sounded like a disaster waiting to happen.

"I'm calling Haley," Spencer said.

"What—no, Spence," Peter protested. "We can do this ourselves."

Spencer pulled his phone out of his pocket. "Her dad is a lumberjack," he said decidedly. "She'll know how to do this *safely*."

Peter rolled his eyes, then turned to Cassandra as Spencer disappeared down the hall. "Your boyfriend is a pansy."

"I prefer the term 'intelligent,'" she replied with a glimmer of humor in her eyes.

Ignoring her quip, Peter looked up at Connor. "You got any traditions to add to our list?"

Resigned to this hair-brained scheme, Connor shrugged. "Not really. My family didn't celebrate Christmas like everyone else. And what we *did* do, I'm not interested in reminiscing on."

"Fair enough. How about you, Cass? You and Diane have any fun traditions?"

"We did, actually," Cassandra said, opening one of the boxes. "Every year, we'd make eggnog and then drink it while opening gifts and reading *A Christmas Carol* to each other on Christmas Eve. I'd always go to Spokane for Christmas Day, but those nights with Diane were my favorite part of the season."

"Well then, we gotta do it this year too!" Peter insisted. "What ingredients do you need to make eggnog? Eggs, right?"

Cassandra smirked. "You have to age it, Peter. Diane and I would make it three weeks early."

Peter waved a dismissive hand. "Sure, maybe that's ideal, but we'll age it for the next four days, and it'll be better than *not* having it."

Cassandra shrugged in acceptance.

"Cool." Peter slapped Connor's arm. "Come on then, golden god. We've got a grocery list to make."

With one last long-suffering look at Cassandra, Connor followed Peter into the kitchen.

CHAPTER FOUR

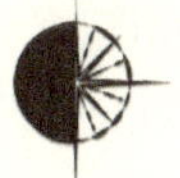

Spencer

Haley was more than happy to join them on their tree excursion. "Aaron and I went with both our families to get trees a couple of weeks ago," she said over the phone. "I think he has off tomorrow morning, so he can join us too. Why'd you wait this long?"

"Uh . . ." Spencer glanced up as Peter and Connor entered the kitchen, headed for the pantry. "Blame it on work."

Haley gave a short, dry chuckle. "Yeah, Owen said it's been nonstop. All right, we'll meet you at Occasus around nine o'clock tomorrow morning. Sound good?"

"That's great. Thanks."

After hanging up, Spencer left the kitchen to join Cassandra back in the living room. She'd already made her way through most of one box. Bunting, candlesticks, boxes of vintage ornaments, dried pinecones, and bags of lights lay across the couches and coffee table in a decidedly organized fashion.

Leaning against the doorframe where the French doors hung open between the living room and office, Spencer smiled. Cassandra tucked some hair behind her ear as she dug through the box. She was a walking contradiction in her all-black outfit and wistful smile as she pulled out a gold, hammered Christmas star. He could almost imagine her in a Dickensian dress, preparing for an 1880s Christmas party.

"You know that's weird, right?" Cassandra said suddenly. She set the star on the couch next to the boxes of ornaments. Then she smirked at him. "Watching me silently."

Spencer returned the wry grin. "Not at all," he said. "Just admiring your organizational skills."

"Ha, ha." She draped a strand of stuffed stars next to the bunting. "Diane never put things away with any sense of order, just wherever they could fit. Now, I'm making our lives easier for later."

"Mm-hm. Well," Spencer motioned to the office behind him, "while you do that, would you mind if I finish up the special? I've only got a few paragraphs left to edit, and then I can join you."

Cassandra waved him off. "Take your time," she said, then frowned at the next box. "This is a mess."

Chuckling silently to himself, Spencer took his seat back at the desk. He rubbed the base of his head where he still felt the occasional pressure from his head wound after the attack at the Veil and opened his laptop to reread the last few lines, picking back up in Wenzel and Frankly's story. After weeks of not writing a word, Spencer and Peter had struggled to get back into the habit. It felt so inconsequential in the face of Druids and Spectrals, the Warden and the town. But Cassandra had been insistent, and they'd needed the reminder of their goals.

So, he and Peter had decided on their final episode for the year. They'd already had a good start, having planned the Christmas Special back when they first made it to DeVerre. It was going to be a sizeable post— approximately ten thousand words long versus their regular two thousand-word episodes. One last hurrah before *Wenzel & Frankly* became a series of novels rather than a serial on a blog.

Reviewing the final scene, Spencer made the minor adjustments that Peter suggested in his previous read-through. They were wrapping up the serial with a teaser for the overarching plot that would unfold throughout the series. Though they'd spent most of their writing career letting the story tell itself without planning ahead, they'd begun to change that.

During Peter's captivity, he'd said he had tons of time to think, so he came up with lots of ideas for what was to come. They'd compiled those ideas, along with others, into a document, developing them into a somewhat clear storyline that would span five books. Maybe more if things went well.

"You done yet?" Cassandra asked teasingly as she stepped into the room.

Spencer typed in a couple more words, then turned to her with a smile. "Almost."

"Mm. Well, take a break, okay?" She moved forward, hands hidden behind her back, and nodded to where he sat. "I need to be there."

Furrowing his brow, Spencer tried to catch a glimpse of what she was hiding, but she moved. "Why?" he asked.

"Wouldn't you like to know?" She tipped up her chin. "Move."

Chuckling at her playful mood, Spencer rose from his chair. Then, Cassandra scooted the low-backed rolling chair over so that she could carefully step on it and then the desk. Spencer would have asked what she was doing, but she quickly reached up and tied something to the chandelier that hung over his desk.

"There," Cassandra said and jumped down. She motioned to his chair. "Sit down."

Spencer didn't listen but stared up at the dried piece of mistletoe hanging from the antique chandelier. He turned to her, raising his brow.

With a knowing grin, Cassandra crossed her arms. "It's a tradition," she defended. "Diane would always hang it above her desk because that's what Liam used to do. She said he would take every opportunity to interrupt her while she worked to kiss her. Hanging it up after he died was her way of keeping him as a part of the season."

Spencer set a hand on the back of his chair, eyes flicking up toward the mistletoe. "And this is only to keep the memory of their love alive, right?" he joked.

She winked. "Of course."

Spencer took his seat, scooting back to sit before his laptop.

Cassandra swept up behind him, wrapped her arms around his chest, and planted a kiss on his cheek. "Merry Christmas," she whispered.

His heart warmed brightly. "From Liam and Diane?"

"And me," she said.

Spencer squeezed her hand, then turned to look up at her. "It would have been nice to have Christmas with you and Diane. I wish she had invited us."

"I do too," Cassandra said with a sigh. She pulled back, moving to lean against the desk. "And honestly, I wish I had returned to DeVerre sooner so I could have met Liam too. Everything Diane told me about him . . . Well, he actually sounds kind of like you."

"Oh, yeah?" That surprised Spencer somehow.

Cassandra nodded. "She said he was quiet and serious, but a total romantic at heart."

"I wouldn't say I'm a romantic."

"As your girlfriend, I have evidence to the contrary."

Spencer rolled his eyes but continued to smile at her. "I would have liked to meet them too," he said. "Back when we first moved here, Anna said they were a cute couple. Completely in love even after decades of marriage."

"They were," Cassandra said. "I always felt so bad for Diane, being a widow. She would talk about Liam as though he were still here, and sometimes, she'd get this far-off look in her eyes as though she were reliving a memory with him. It was really heartbreaking and adorable all at the same time."

The romance between Liam and Diane Larkin reminded Spencer of his parents. David and Mallory had had the same deep connection, always happiest when they were together. And Spencer had always dreamed of finding the same kind of love, though he'd somehow doubted the possibility of it until he'd met Cassandra.

Looking up at her, Spencer asked one of the questions that he'd wondered about the Larkins since he and Peter inherited the estate. "Do you know why they didn't have kids?"

Cassandra shook her head. "No, actually. Diane never talked about it, and—well, that can be a rather touchy subject, so I never felt right asking about it. But when one of the women at the church was struggling with her early pregnancy, Diane said something about feeling bad for her, unable to comprehend what it was like to be pregnant. So I just assumed that they either didn't want kids or couldn't have them."

"Hm." Spencer played with one of the pens on the desk. "Do you want kids?"

Cassandra's eyes widened a fraction before she schooled her expression. "Well, being the Vessel, I sort of *have* to have a kid to carry on the bloodline," she said. "But yes, even if the Warden wouldn't require that of me, I've always wanted children."

"Child*ren*? How many?"

She wouldn't meet his gaze as she said, "Three. Maybe four. It was just me and Ike growing up, and that always felt . . . small, somehow. I think I want a bigger family." She paused, fiddling with the hem of her sleeve. She looked at him between her lashes. "Do you want kids?"

"Yes," he said without hesitation. "Though I imagined having two, probably because it was just Pete and me growing up. But I think more would be nice."

She gave a nervous smile, head dipped.

Spencer knew her worried silences now, and he reached across to tap her arm. "You know, we probably shouldn't be weird about this stuff," he said. "We are dating, and serious subjects like this are sort of necessary to discuss."

"Oh, I know," she said with a half-hearted shrug. "I just don't want you to think I'm pressuring you or anything."

"I don't," he promised. "And you're not going to scare me off. We can talk about serious, future topics like this and make sure we want the same things. And in the meantime, let's just assume we're gonna stay together, okay?"

Chewing on the inside of her lip, Cassandra eyed him curiously. "That would mean assuming we're going to get married."

He smirked. "That's sort of the point of dating, isn't it?"

She stared at him with something like awe in her expression. "You're a really good guy, Spencer," she said tenderly. "Like, a surprisingly sweet, honorable guy."

He dipped his chin, happily embarrassed by her compliment. "I just try to do what I think would make my dad proud."

"Well," she pushed away from the desk, leaning down toward him, "I think he'd be *very* proud of you." Then she kissed him under the mistletoe.

Spencer thought it was meant to be one idle kiss by the way she began to pull back. Neither of them was satisfied with that. The one kiss turned into another, more passionate one. And then another. And another.

Soon, Cassandra set her hands on his face, and Spencer's hands were on her hips. She'd bent at the waist, coming to stand closer to where he sat in the desk chair. But just as he considered getting up to make the kisses easier, Cassandra settled herself on his lap.

As the kiss deepened, extending for heated seconds, Spencer's whole body tingled. His hands skimmed her sides as her arms wrapped around his neck. Pulling back from the kiss just enough to whisper, he asked, "Is this okay?"

Cassandra's fingers tangled in the grown-out ends of his hair. "I'm the one who sat down, Spence," she murmured.

"Well, yeah." A shiver ran down his spine as she trailed kisses along his cheek. His grip tightened on the curve of her waist. "That doesn't mean it's the smartest idea."

Her amused reply tickled his ear. "Are you calling me stupid?"

Wonderfully agitated by her teasing, Spencer tugged her closer. "Never," he said just before capturing her mouth in a deep kiss that sent a buzzing warmth into his toes.

They descended into a spiral of each other's embrace for several magical moments before a giant, annoyed sigh hissed through the air.

Cassandra pulled back, turning so that they could both see Peter and Connor standing in the hall. Peter wore a bland, perturbed expression, while Connor rubbed the back of his neck, clearly on the verge of laughter. Still, Cassandra didn't get up from Spencer's lap.

"Look," Peter said. "I get it. You're still in that fun honeymoon stage or whatever. I've given you a month to enjoy it. Now," he leveled Spencer with a flat stare, "you need to stop making out in public. I don't wanna see that."

Spencer ducked his head, feeling like a chastised teen. Cassandra pressed her lips together, rising at last.

"Better in public than in private," Connor quipped. "They can only go so far when you're lurking around every corner."

"I don't lurk," Peter returned, then paused. He quirked his brow and let out a hum of thought. "You know, Zeus, you've got a point." He turned back to Spencer and Cassandra then. "Carry on. Just . . . keep it to a minimum, yeah?"

"Got it," Spencer said sourly.

Peter shot him a finger gun, then pointed to the door. "All right, well, we're headed out. We'll be back in an hour or so, and I expect to find this place decked out in holiday cheer and not with you guys on the couch, okay?"

Spencer threw a pen at him. "Get out."

Connor sniggered while Peter winked at Spencer. Then, they left.

Cassandra had drifted toward the living room once more, an amused if bashful expression on her face. "Sorry," she murmured.

"For what?" Spencer asked.

She gestured toward the front door. "For the—I'm not very good with . . ." She blew out an exasperated breath. "I've never had a relationship like this."

Spencer's brow furrowed, unsure what she meant.

"And it's hard knowing where the line is," she said, then grimaced. "Or when Peter's gonna walk into the room."

He laughed then. "I'm pretty sure that's a uniquely 'us' situation."

She made an overdramatically annoyed face.

Spencer cleared his throat, attempting to hear the words she'd left unsaid. "Are you saying that you've never had a serious relationship? Or that you've never made out with someone before me?"

A soft flush came to her cheeks. "Both."

"Hm." Spencer pressed his lips together, considering the beautiful woman who stood before him.

The answer surprised Spencer. He'd known she hadn't had many relationships through the years, but who *wouldn't* want to date Cassandra? And while he hadn't expected that she would go around kissing any guy who called her pretty, he was surprised by her lack of physical experience. She was an affectionate person in general, and she'd been readily welcoming of his advances over the past month. They hadn't gone farther than lingering kisses, gentle touches, and occasional cuddles, nor did he have any interest in pursuing more before marriage. However, Cassandra had never even flinched when he touched her more intimately than he would anyone else. And he'd assumed that was because she'd experienced those sorts of things with Jacob.

"Well," Spencer said at last, "I haven't either. In case that wasn't obvious."

Cassandra narrowed her gaze, a slight smirk on her lips. "Had a serious relationship or made out with someone?"

He dipped his chin in a mock bow. "Both."

"Lucky me."

"Other way around." Spencer motioned to the laptop, still open on his desk. "Now, I've *really* gotta finish this special. Give me fifteen more minutes?"

Cassandra began to back away, the almost dimple on her cheek readily displayed as she smiled. "Anything for you, Frankly."

Spencer shook his head, turning back to the computer. Cassandra had begun calling him that from time to time after he'd confirmed that, yes, he had created Serene Verlice, the undercover monster hunter and love interest of Dr. Charles Frankly, based on many of Cassandra's attributes. From then on, he could always pin her use of "Frankly" to when she felt particularly happy in their relationship.

Attempting to get back into the story, Spencer sent a sidelong glance at Cassandra, back to perusing the Christmas decorations in the living room. He looked forward to celebrating the holiday with her. Having a girlfriend was a unique experience for him in general. Having one at Christmastime was especially enjoyable. All the traditions he'd enjoyed as a kid would be even more meaningful with her at his side.

Spencer tapped the keyboard thoughtfully. Sharing traditions wasn't the only thing he anticipated this holiday. That phone call from Allen Clement had been fortuitous. Spencer had been hoping to meet the Clements for a while now. When Cassandra said he was honorable, she didn't realize that he was also somewhat old-fashioned. Though he didn't think he needed to ask her dad for permission to date her, he did want to make the man aware of his intentions.

The problem was that Spencer hadn't met Allen or Julianne yet. And he hadn't known how to make that happen. Until today.

Spencer knew Cassandra didn't have the same kind of relationship with her parents that he had with his. The Clements had been unsupportive and hurtful. They didn't deserve her goodness or her trust. But they were still her family, and no matter how screwed up they might be, they loved her. And every parent wanted to know that their child was cared for. Truly and genuinely cared for.

This trip to Spokane was the perfect time for Spencer to prove himself—to Cassandra *and* her parents.

With a smile at his secret thoughts, Spencer forced himself to read the last few paragraphs. He could think about his plans later. It didn't matter that he and Cassandra had only been dating a month, or that they'd only met one month before that. These two months were enough for him to know how he felt. And he was ready to tell her.

But first, he wanted to meet her parents and assure them that no matter what—whether or not they accepted him and her choice to stay in DeVerre—he would love their daughter for the rest of his life.

CHAPTER FIVE

Peter

The DeVerre grocery store was small but ample enough to provide the basics and then some. Most importantly, it would have all the ingredients they needed to make their Christmas successful.

"So," Connor said, a hint bitterly as they worked their way into the store, "what all's on this list of Christmas activities of yours?"

"Oh, you know, the classics," Peter said, leaning on the cart's handle. "Getting the tree, making some ornaments, decorating said tree. Making cookies, wrapping gifts, eating way too much food. Drinking hot cocoa and watching movies. Which reminds me, we need a TV."

Connor glanced down at him. "You don't have a television?"

Peter shrugged. "Diane wasn't a fan, apparently. And Spence and I haven't exactly had time to binge a rewatch of *Numbers*."

Connor let out an indifferent hum.

After tossing two boxes of popcorn into the cart, Peter marked it off the list in his notebook.

"Why don't you use a phone like a normal person?" Connor asked, watching the process.

Peter continued down the aisle, unbothered. "Electronics are too distracting. I can't get things done if I try to do them digitally. It's a trick I learned in college. People always told me I had ADHD, but I had this professor who suggested I try working analogously, and it worked. Without the distraction of the internet and flashy lights, I could actually get stuff done. Turns out, I *am* hyperactive, but I'm not disordered."

Connor scoffed good-naturedly. "You sure about that?"

Peter smirked but kept his focus on his list as he directed them to the next aisle.

"So," Connor continued, "that's all? We're gonna watch movies and eat?"

"And decorate the tree." Peter snapped his fingers. "Which reminds me: we've gotta be at the Christmas tree lighting in the plaza tonight."

"I can't believe they're still doing that."

"The town needs some cheer, man."

"People died."

Peter frowned at him. "Give them a break. We all deal with grief in our own ways."

Connor was quiet for several moments as they walked down the next aisle. Peter assumed he was thinking about his personal grief. After weeks of talking on the phone, they'd become a strange level of close. Peter wouldn't begin to assume that he knew what was going on in Connor's mind, but somehow, he could see the trauma that marred his heart plainly on his face.

Letting the man ruminate in peace, Peter marked off the next item on his list before stopping in front of the baking supplies.

"Did you know that Anna's parents are coming into town?" Connor asked suddenly.

Peter blinked at the rows of sugar. Slowly, he turned to face Connor. "When?"

"Tomorrow."

His heart skipped a beat. "That soon, huh?"

"Yeah."

"Mm." Peter grabbed bags of white and brown sugar and dumped them into the cart.

As Peter started off again, Connor muttered, "They want to meet with us."

Peter grimaced with the guilt churning inside of him. He didn't want to deal with Anna's parents right now. They were supposed to be celebrating Christmas, getting a much-needed break. And now, they'd have to explain to the Lamberts how they'd gotten their daughter killed.

Glancing up at Connor, he asked, "To get answers?"

"Yeah."

"Cool." He scratched his head. "How'd you—?"

"Aaron told me when I got into town."

Peter nodded, leaning heavily on the cart's handle.

"He asked if tomorrow night would be good," Connor said.

"Uh . . . Well, I'm working at the tavern tomorrow night," Peter said. "But they could meet us there, I guess."

Peter had started picking up shifts at The Glass Tavern in Anna's place. While he wasn't sure she'd *want* her old job when she came back to life, he'd taken it as a way to help facilitate the ruse of her temporary absence. As he'd been a bartender since college before coming to DeVerre, it was an easy job to pick up, and it met the provisions of Diane's will. Not that that mattered much anymore. If things went well, even if they lost the house to Cassandra, she'd be married to Spencer, and the house would remain in the family anyway.

"Don't you think that'd be weird?" Connor asked, bringing Peter's wandering thoughts back to the moment. "I mean, that's where Anna . . ."

"We don't have much other choice," Peter said. "I'm on the closing shift."

"Couldn't you trade?"

"In less than twenty-four hours? After everything that happened, there's only, like, four other waiters left. And Haley's one of them. Who do you think is going to be available at such short notice, the week of Christmas?"

Connor sighed. "Fine, whatever. I guess we can ask."

"I'll talk to Aaron tonight at the tree lighting," Peter promised. "If they don't want to meet at the tavern tomorrow, we can see about meeting up on Wednesday."

Connor picked at the boxes of stuffing on the shelf.

"Something else bothering you, man?" Peter prompted.

"It's nothing," he muttered.

Peter studied him for a moment, then took a wild stab. "You nervous about seeing them again?"

Connor's silence was confirmation enough.

"Did Aaron say if they specifically asked to talk with you too?"

"Yeah," he said. "Though apparently, they think you and Spencer are of more interest."

"Ah." Peter didn't like that one bit. But he chose to focus on Connor in this moment. "So, you think they're pissed at you and won't forgive you when you try to apologize?"

"Something like that," he said begrudgingly.

Peter had no clue what the Lambert parents were like. He wasn't even sure he'd heard their names before. He had no idea if they were the sort to hold grudges, and he couldn't fault Connor for fearing that outcome. After all, the guy had lied to them for over twenty years.

Shrugging nonchalantly, Peter tried to brush off the concern. "I'm sure it'll be fine, man. These are Anna's parents we're talking about. They can't be douchebags, can they?"

"Of course not!" Connor said defensively. "Andrew and Aimee are the most incredible parents in the world. But that's the point: they care about their children more than anything." He lowered his voice then, adding, "And I got their daughter killed."

"Well . . ." Peter paused. He supposed Connor *had* gotten Anna killed by spurning Lily. But he didn't think agreeing would help anything, so he changed his argument. "Okay, so, yeah, they probably deserve to be a bit upset with you. But they're *Anna's parents*. If *she* could forgive you—along with Aaron, Ava, Haley, and Owen—then surely her parents can too."

Connor was silent.

"I'm not saying it's going to be easy," Peter admitted. "I just . . . I dunno. If her parents are anything like their kids, then I don't see them holding this against you. Not when you're doing everything you can to . . ." He glanced around the store, then whispered, "You know."

"Maybe," Connor mumbled, clearly unconvinced.

Peter sighed, knowing he wouldn't make any more progress. "Come on," he said. "Let's get these last few things and get home."

After picking up the rest of their groceries, they drove over to the general store to purchase a television. It was a small, older model due to DeVerre's limited supply, but it had internet capabilities, so it would do.

When they got home, Peter was pleased to find that Spencer and Cassandra had indeed decked the very halls of Occasus. Garland trimmed the stair rail and fireplace mantels. Spencer stood on a short ladder, hanging bunting from the doorframe between the entry and living room. The vintage decor made Peter feel as though he were stepping into *A Christmas Carol*.

At Spencer's side, Cassandra handed him pieces of tape, one at a time. She eyed Peter and Connor as they stomped their feet on the mat outside, arms laden with bags. "You buy out the entire grocery store?" she asked.

"He insisted it was necessary," Connor grumbled.

Peter didn't bother replying. He smiled up at Spencer as he moved past. "Lookin' good up there, Poirot."

Cassandra gave Spencer's leg a nudge. "He is, isn't he?"

"Shut up, both of you," Spencer said, eyes fixed on his task. "This whole thing is about to fall, and I've used an entire roll of tape already."

"Oh, hang on," Peter exclaimed. "I've got some Command hooks in here somewhere."

Hurrying off to the kitchen, Peter deposited the bags. He rummaged through, found the hooks, returned them to Spencer, then put away the groceries. Connor dropped off his bags, too, then headed back out to get the TV.

Once they stored the food supplies, they temporarily propped the television on a low bookshelf in the living room. "It doesn't look the nicest," Peter said as they surveyed their handiwork, "but it'll do for the holiday. We can pack it away after."

"Honestly," Spencer added, working on hanging another string of bunting between the office and living room, "I've liked not having the distraction."

"Me too," Peter admitted. He glanced out the window at the low-hanging sun. "What time was the tree lighting again?"

"Usually, it's around six," Cassandra said. "The sun's typically gone down enough by then."

"Then we've got like, twenty minutes," Connor warned.

Peter grimaced. "Guess we'd better get going."

Thankfully, none of them had to do much to get ready. Once Spencer and Cassandra had put on their shoes, they all bundled up and got in the Jeep. "We'll have to park at the chapel," Connor warned. "People always get there early, and they block off the plaza."

Sure enough, when they walked onto Harmony Plaza from the chapel's lot, Cassandra's detail straggling behind at a respectful distance, they found the small square near bursting with people. There were small hot chocolate and snack stands, as well as a kids' craft area off to the side. They caught sight of Haley helping with the kids and waved to her.

Lights were strung up along nearly all the businesses around the plaza, wreaths on every door and window. Even the police station had decorated its windows with plastic stickers and lights. An unlit Christmas tree soared into the sky next to the town hall, nearly as tall as the bell tower on the whitewashed government building. With the snow covering the ground and roofs, it looked like a scene straight out of a Christmas movie.

"Not gonna lie," Peter said to Spencer as they wove their way through the crowd. "We've never had a Christmas that felt so Christmas-y."

Smiling, Spencer nodded in agreement.

The gentle tinkle of Christmas music played from a large speaker on a platform by the town hall. Owen stood at its side, talking with Rhader and a few other Warden officials. As the interim mayor, Owen oversaw events like this. As a Warden member, he also influenced the organization's decisions. Though he hadn't wanted the role, he'd taken to it like a Varon to wielding.

Not far from the platform, Peter saw Ava and Aaron talking with Tom Garnier, the marshal. He nudged Spencer's shoulder and pointed out their friends. They headed over, greeting the Lamberts and the marshal. "Good to have you back," Ava said to Connor.

"Thanks," he replied quietly.

"I heard you're taking a vacation," Tom said to Peter, Spencer, and Cassandra. "Good for you. Those people don't let up, do they?"

Cassandra shrugged. "They didn't fight us on the break," she said.

"Though it looks like your detail isn't easing up," Aaron noted with a nod to the Warden members following them.

Peter and Spencer shared a look as Cassandra sighed. "A perk of the job," she said, keeping her voice low.

The marshal let out a flat grunt, then excused himself. He scanned the plaza as though looking for signs of trouble as he made his way toward his wife and sons. Stephanie Garnier laughed merrily as their late-teen boys chased one another with fists of snow, Tom joining in as he approached.

Peter smiled at the marshal's family, wondering if that's how the Collins family might have looked if they'd grown up in DeVerre.

"Owen is going to be busy during the lighting," Ava said, drawing his attention back to their small group. She wore a thick, woven scarf around her neck and had her hands tucked into her mustard-yellow coat's pockets. Even without its baggy fit, she still wasn't showing signs of her pregnancy. At least, not that Peter had noticed. "But he'll be free shortly after, and we're planning to head back to the house for a game of rummy. You all are welcome to join."

Peter looked at his brother and friends. "Sounds good to me," he said.

Upon Spencer, Cassandra, and Connor's agreement, the plans were made.

"Great," Aaron said, in his usual serious tone. "Did Connor mention tomorrow night to you guys?"

Peter snorted at his direct manner, then turned to Spencer and Cassandra, both wearing surprised expressions. "Their parents are getting in town tomorrow," he explained. "And they want to meet up."

Understanding and hesitation widened their eyes as Peter turned back to Aaron. "Yeah, we're good to meet," he said. "Though I'm working at the tavern, so it'll have to be there. If that isn't too weird a place to meet up."

"Why would it be weird?" Ava asked.

"Uh . . ." Peter glanced at Connor. Then he shrugged. "'Cause Anna worked there."

She raised a brow. "The Glass Tavern has been around for nearly one hundred years. My parents have frequented the restaurant for far longer than Anna has been alive. And," she gave him a pointed look, "there's no reason they wouldn't want to go there now."

Peter realized then that she was right—they couldn't show their discomfort with those sorts of things. After all, if Anna was alive as they'd told the town, why should it bother them to go where she used to go? They weren't grieving. Their friend had simply gone out of town for a while.

"Fair enough," Peter said, shivering as a cold breeze cut through. "You know why they want to talk with us, exactly? I mean, I assume they want more information, but . . . What can we tell them that you guys haven't yet?"

"Honestly?" Aaron shrugged. "I'm not sure. Mom is a lot like Ava, though. She likes facts and details. If something doesn't make sense to her, she doesn't leave it alone until she figures it out."

Peter glanced at Ava. "Then why didn't she ever pursue knowledge about the spirit world?"

"Same reason I didn't," Ava said. "We believed it was dangerous and that it needed to be forgotten. That meant leaving well enough alone."

"Huh. I guess that makes sense."

The crowd around them began to turn, and Cassandra nudged Peter's arm to draw his attention to the stage. Owen stepped up to the microphone, giving one of his reserved smiles as he greeted the town. The reverend, Sam Chapelle, stood at his side.

"Welcome to DeVerre's annual Christmas tree lighting," Owen said, his calm tone soothing through the speakers. "We're grateful to all of you who showed up and pitched in to help make this possible. After a hard year, we believe moments like these are a great way to remind ourselves of what matters most: family, togetherness, and God's peace."

As he spoke, the plaza fell silent, listening intently. The frigid air swirled through the crowd, and Cassandra shifted closer to Spencer. Haley snuck up behind Aaron, slipping her arms around his waist. He reached back and wrapped his arm around her.

A tinge of jealousy swelled in Peter's chest, longing for the day when he had someone too. But then he caught a glimpse of the tension in Connor's jaw, and he realized he didn't have much to be upset about. Maybe he was alone, but he hadn't lost the woman he loved.

Owen turned the mic over to Sam, who stepped up to pray over the evening, thanking God for the gift of His Son. Peter told himself to focus on what he did have rather than what he didn't: He had Spencer, the most amazing brother in the world, and an incredible best friend in Cassandra. He had the Bernards, the Lamberts, and Connor. He had his mom, even if she was states away. He had Occasus, he had a lineage, and as the Varon ring on his finger reminded him, he had the power to care for those he loved.

Everyone around Peter began counting down.

"Ten . . . Nine . . . Eight . . ."

Peter smiled, looking up at the star on the top of the tree. Yes, he had quite a lot to be thankful for this Christmas season.

"Seven . . . Six . . . Five . . ."

Even if there were still questions, even if Anna was gone, they had hope.

"Four . . . Three . . . Two . . ."

Peter put his arm around Spencer, joining the final countdown. "One!"

The glimmer of lights buzzed to life. A golden glow filled the plaza, shining in the oversized ornaments on the tree. And at the top of the pine, the Christmas star shone a brilliant silver, like the star above Bethlehem, guiding the wise men to the true meaning of the season, to the greatest gift of love there ever was.

Applause erupted around the plaza, and Peter's smile grew, his heart filling as he squeezed Spencer closer, shaking him excitedly. On Spencer's other side, arm tucked around her, Cassandra laughed at Peter's antics. With Aaron's arm draped over her shoulder, Haley held Ava's hand. Owen smiled at them from the platform.

Seeing Connor standing to the side, isolated from everyone else, Peter reached over. "Get over here, Zeus," he said, tugging firmly on his arm.

Peter tossed his arm up to Connor's towering shoulders, forcing the guy to stoop. "Merry Christmas!" Peter shouted, not caring that he looked like an idiot or that Connor was trying to shrug him off.

"Merry Christmas!" Shouts rang back to Peter, the people of DeVerre cheering along with him as they celebrated the hope and joy the season brought to their healing hearts.

Yes, Peter thought, the town was healing. And this Christmas would help with that.

CHAPTER SIX

Cassandra

The late-morning sun glinted off the iced-over trees in Blackwood Forest as Cassandra, Spencer, Peter, Connor, Haley, and Aaron trudged through the woods. The snow crunched under their boots while the clear, white-blue sky stretched overhead. A cold breeze drifted through the trees, but the sunlight lent a pleasant warmth to the light surrounding them.

Though Cassandra had helped Diane decorate for Christmas, she'd never actually gone out to chop down a tree. Diane had always hired one of the young men from the church to take on the task. Now, Cassandra wondered if it might have been one of Haley's brothers.

"What about this one?" Haley suggested, drifting toward a hollow in the trees. A smattering of pines created a pretty vignette, the sun flaring mystically between them.

Turning to see the hollow, Peter's expression pinched strangely. "Ah, no—no, I—hey, what about these over here?" He hurried over to a squat but full tree on the opposite side of the clearing. "This one looks like it could use a good home."

Cassandra and Spencer shared a look, but the others didn't seem to notice Peter's odd behavior.

"That's an ugly tree," Connor said flatly.

"But this one isn't bad," Aaron said, inspecting a pine a few trees removed. "It's a little lopsided, but we can fix that with the right base set up. You did get a stand, right?"

"Oh, uh—" Peter scratched the back of his head through his beanie. "No, I didn't. We grew up with fake trees, so I didn't think about it."

Cassandra lifted her brow in surprise. "With all your family's over-the-top traditions, I would have expected you to get a real tree," she remarked.

"Yeah, well, Dad was the one who put the lights on," Spencer said. "And he got tired of restringing them every year."

Cassandra couldn't blame David Collins for that practicality.

She turned back to the other men. "Diane kept her tree stand in the shed," she told them. "I saw it when we grabbed the supplies this morning."

"Great!" Peter patted the tree proudly. "Let's get this bad boy back home, shall we?"

With Haley's close guidance, Aaron and Peter set to work. The tree was felled with relative ease under her direction. Then, they bound up their haul to make it easier to carry, and the men lugged it back through the forest.

Cassandra and Haley drifted along at the back of the group. She hadn't spent much time with the bubbly blonde one-on-one, and now, she found she didn't know what to say to her. Haley was Cassandra's near opposite. The young woman wore a light pink knit cap with a fluffy white pom-pom. Her winter coat was a creamy ivory, and her boots were a pretty sage green. She looked bright and cheery, while Cassandra was a dark shadow in the forest.

Still, Cassandra wanted to connect with the woman. She'd concluded that her over-confident, standoffish demeanor had likely kept her and Diane from finding answers in the past. If Cassandra had tried to make friends in DeVerre—if she hadn't been so dreadfully stubborn, sure that the townspeople would hate her on principle—she might have helped keep Diane alive.

Clearing her throat, Cassandra gave Haley a timid smile. "How, uh— how's wedding planning going?" she asked.

"Oh, it's good," Haley said, her bright blue eyes almost sparkling. "We haven't gotten much done, and we can't really set a date until we get Anna back, but we've got some good plans in place for when the time does come."

Cassandra hadn't even thought about the fact that Anna's death would forestall Aaron and Haley's wedding. Then she realized how ridiculous that was because, of course, they wouldn't get married without Anna there. Assuming they actually could resurrect her. . . .

"Makes sense," Cassandra said. Then she bit her lip. She'd never had friends like this, and she didn't know what to talk about concerning weddings. Oh, she'd been to them, but even when her brother got married, she didn't do much but show up to stand as one of the bridesmaids at her sister-in-law's side.

"We have decided on the bridal party, though," Haley said without Cassandra's prompting. "Aaron's already asked Owen to be his best man, and don't tell, but he plans to ask Peter, Spencer, and Connor all to stand up with him too, along with my brothers."

That surprised Cassandra. She didn't know Aaron any better than she knew Haley, but she assumed that he had lifelong friends within DeVerre that he'd ask first. Though she supposed he wasn't nearly as sociable as his fiancée and younger sister.

"My lips are sealed," Cassandra promised.

Haley's smile turned demure. She played with the pink and cream tassels on her scarf. "It'll be a big bridal party, but we couldn't imagine not having the day without our favorite people at our sides," she continued. "Of course, Anna will be the maid of honor, and I've already asked Ava to be a bridesmaid. She's taking the job very seriously."

Cassandra couldn't help chuckling. "I can imagine. I bet she's creating a spreadsheet for you."

Haley laughed too. "Something like that," she said and ducked under a low-hanging branch. "I don't have any sisters-in-law yet, but Devon is dating Bailey Durand, and he's planning to propose once she graduates in the spring, so I'm going to ask her while she's in town for Christmas. And . . ."

Cassandra turned to Haley in her pause.

The young woman grinned broadly. "I wanted to ask you to be a bridesmaid too," she said.

Cassandra blanched. "What?"

"I know we haven't been friends long," Haley said gently. "You never really gave Anna or me a chance to get to know you in the past. But after everything we've been through . . ." She shrugged. "I think saving the town from Druids together has officially given us a bond that others can't really compete with."

Speechless, Cassandra's hands trembled at her sides. In her entire life, she'd longed for friendships deep enough and connections rich enough to be considered vital to other people's lives. But after twenty-nine years of feeling impossibly separate, decidedly unwanted . . . Cassandra had nearly given up hope of creating any lasting bond.

Now, she found herself coming to a stop in the woods to stare at Haley Roux, who smiled over at her with a knowing look in her kind gaze.

"Are you sure?" Cassandra asked quietly.

Haley nodded. "I have a feeling that we're going to be in each other's lives for a very long time," she said. "And that makes me quite happy."

Inexplicably, Cassandra felt tears coming to her eyes. "I'm not very good at being a friend."

"That's silly," Haley said, then looped her arm through Cassandra's, pulling her back onto the path toward Occasus. "You're loyal, passionate, and dependable. I don't think you have it in you to be a bad friend. Plus, you're undeniably cool."

An embarrassed laugh slipped out of Cassandra, but she couldn't come up with any witty reply. Not in the face of such kindness.

"You haven't answered me," Haley commented. Then she tipped her head to the side. "Though I guess I didn't properly ask. Cass, would you be one of my bridesmaids?"

Heart warmer than it had been in a long time, Cassandra walked in step with Haley through the snow. "I'd be honored."

~

"I always thought Linus didn't get enough credit," Peter said, sitting on the couch as he threaded popcorn onto a string.

Cassandra glanced over at the television, *Charlie Brown Christmas* playing in the background as they decorated the tree. She looped the lights around another branch. "What are you talking about?" she said. "Linus is everyone's favorite."

Connor swore under his breath, shaking out his hand. "I hate hot glue guns," he muttered.

"That's because you're using it wrong," Spencer commented, sitting across the coffee table from him on the floor.

After bringing the tree in, they'd invited Aaron and Haley to join them to make ornaments, but the couple had to pick his parents up at the airport in Spokane, so it was back to the four of them. A smattering of felt, thread, and other crafting bobbles covered the coffee table's top. Cassandra had deftly avoided making her ornament yet, letting the guys take their turns first. She'd never been one for crafts, and she didn't know how to tell Spencer that sewing beads onto stars sounded like a particularly heinous form of torture.

So, while Connor and Spencer worked on their ornaments and Peter made a popcorn garland, Cassandra opted to begin stringing the lights on the tree.

"Done," Spencer said, holding up a small felt star he'd embroidered with metallic thread.

"Impressive work, J.B.," Peter said, then tossed a piece of popcorn into his mouth. "You're a regular Betsy Ross."

Spencer rolled his eyes and stood. He stepped up to Cassandra's side. "Want to trade?" he asked.

"Oh, no, I'm okay," she promised, hoping to avoid making a fool out of herself. She brandished the lights at him. "I can finish up."

"You sure?"

"Definitely."

Spencer shrugged, then returned to the couch to sit at Peter's side. "We're going to run out of popcorn if you keep eating it like that," he commented.

Peter waved him off. "Why do you think I bought two packs?"

As Connor hissed from burning himself again, Spencer reached over to help him out. Together, they finished his ornament, and Peter completed stringing the popcorn garland shortly before Cassandra evenly distributed the last of the lights through the tree. While the guys surveyed their work, Cassandra pulled out Diane's old ornaments.

"Here," she said, hoping to keep Spencer distracted from the fact that she hadn't participated in the craft. "Help me with these, would you?"

"Absolutely," he said, taking the small box from her.

Together, they started hanging the crocheted angels, stitched doves, golden bells, and dried berries.

As the tallest among them, Connor hooked the last bit of garland around the top of the tree. "I don't know why you guys are doing all this," he said. "We're just going to take it down in a matter of days."

"It's the spirit of the thing, Zeus," Peter said, settling his felt star on the tree, its zig-zag trim unsymmetrical but somehow fitting amongst the vintage ornaments.

"Besides," Spencer added, "we're making memories. And that's really what these things are about anyway."

Cassandra's fingers brushed his as they both reached for another ornament. They shared a smile and went back to work.

Yes, Cassandra thought, Christmas was about making memories. And she was very grateful to be part of Spencer's and Peter's Christmas.

After tree decorating, Peter herded them into the kitchen to make cookies. "The recipes are on the counter," he said, pointing to the island while heading for the pantry. "Read off what we need, and Spence and I can get it out."

"This is a lot of cookies," Cassandra said, looking over the printed recipes. She raised her brow, looking up at Spencer. "Chocolate chip, I understand. But do we really need peanut butter Kiss cookies, gingerbread, *and* . . . whatever mint swirl is?"

"These are the traditional cookies," Peter defended from the pantry. "And it wouldn't be Christmas without decorating a gingerbread."

Spencer stepped up to Cassandra's side, gently taking the recipes from her. "You'll like the mint swirl," he said. "Trust me."

"I'm with Cass," Connor said. "Won't this make, like, hundreds of cookies? There are only four of us."

"Well, that's part of the tradition," Peter said, dropping a massive bag of flour onto the counter. "We always made a whole mountain of cookies, and then took tins of them to our neighbors. Granted," he added with a smirk, "we don't have neighbors up on here on Whitehill. But I was thinking we could take them to the kids this year."

Cassandra raised her chin in understanding.

None of them had to ask what Peter meant by "the kids." After the attack at the Veil a month ago, there were a handful of Druid children who'd lost a parent or been left as orphans. With the Warden's help, they'd managed to get them adopted by family or friends within DeVerre. Families who would raise them in a proper home. Some of the kids were in their mid-to-late teens, old enough to pose a slight threat to the Warden, being nearly of age. But because they had extended family members who weren't Druids within the town, they'd been placed in their care instead of being sent away.

However, many were children under ten. In fact, the youngest Frossard child, Josiah, was only six. The Warden had asked Connor to mentor the boy, who viewed him as somewhat of an idol. While Josiah was placed with his aunt and uncle, Katherine and Jermaine Calderon, they already had two teens and weren't looking to restart their family with a little one. They happily fostered their nephew but were hoping to find a better home for him in the future.

Though the Warden had requested that Connor help ensure the boy was raised right and didn't become embittered by his parents' early deaths, Connor had rejected the role, claiming that he couldn't due to being away at medical school. However, Cassandra thought it had more to do with Connor's struggle to distance himself from his family and their past. She also wondered whether he might feel inadequate, unsure how to influence a child in such an impactful way.

Cassandra could strangely understand Connor better than most. Her family, too, had been full of Druids. There were several Sauveterre children among the orphans. And if she'd been offered a young, impressionable Druid child to foster or mentor, she would balk at the responsibility herself.

Once all the ingredients were pulled together, Peter set them to work. Since they only had one stand mixer, he had Spencer and Cassandra start the gingerbread cookies while he and Connor made icing in a mixing bowl on the island.

Standing side by side, Spencer and Cassandra slowly added the dry ingredients to the wet in the mixer. "I noticed by the way," he said softly, the words only loud enough for her to hear over the whir of the motor.

Cassandra blinked, looking over at him. "What?"

He gave her a dry grin. "You still have to make an ornament."

Pressing her lips together, Cassandra took a deep breath. "I'm not a craft person," she murmured.

"Neither am I," he said, though she begged to differ after seeing his impeccably decorated star. "But that's not the point."

Remembering his speech earlier, Cassandra smirked wryly. "Because memories," she said.

"Exactly."

Cassandra sighed, tapping the back of the bowl to send the last remnants of flour, salt, and baking soda into the mixer. "It's gonna look terrible," she warned.

He nudged her arm teasingly. "It'll look great," he promised. "And if you have trouble, I'll help you out."

She let out an affectionate hum. "That doesn't sound so bad, I guess."

They finished the gingerbread dough and began flouring the counter. Spencer dumped the dough out. He handed Cassandra the rolling pin. "Make sure to flour it," he instructed.

She reached across for the flour bag and rubbed a handful of the powder onto the pin. But as she tried to roll out the cookies, the pin stuck.

Cassandra sighed, grabbing another handful of flour, which puffed out in a cloud around her.

Coming back to her side with the cookie cutters in hand, Spencer grinned. "You need an apron," he commented.

Cassandra looked down to find flour splotched all over her black sweater and jeans. She threw her head back dramatically and heaved an annoyed breath. "Yeah, this isn't for me," she said, then handed Spencer the pin. "I give up."

"It'll wash off," he promised with a chuckle.

"It's fine," she said, then slipped her phone out of her back pocket. "I've got to call my dad anyway."

"Oh." Spencer tapped the side of the pin thoughtfully. "Uh, tell him I said hi. If that wouldn't be weird."

Cassandra gave an amused look. "It would be."

"Right. Forget I said anything then."

She patted his arm, then headed off to the office.

Cassandra dropped into Spencer's desk chair, swiveling as she listened to the phone ring. Her dad answered with an unexpectedly chipper, "Hey, Cassie."

"Uh, hi, Dad. I was just calling to let you know, we've decided that we can come down to Spokane." Cassandra played with one of Spencer's pens absentmindedly. "But we want to attend Christmas Eve service at our church here, and we have plans on Christmas Day, so we need to plan around that."

"That's just fine," Allen said with blatant enthusiasm. "Ike and Sandy are spending Christmas Day with her family anyway. They plan to come over and be with us on Christmas Eve. Would you be willing to come for dinner on the twenty-third and spend the night? We could have a brunch and open gifts in the morning."

Cassandra blinked. She'd been prepared only to have dinner, but she didn't know how to say no to this request. And she did want to see her brother and his family. It'd been more than two months since she'd seen her nephews. "Um, yeah. I'll have to ask Spencer and Peter, but yeah, I think that would be all right," she said cautiously.

"Great! Your room is ready, as always. And we'll make sure the guest room is all set up for them." Allen was quiet for a lingering moment before reluctantly adding, "Unless you want Spencer to stay with you."

Cassandra's heart jolted in shock. "Wha—Dad, no! We're not sleeping together."

"I didn't want to assume," he said, a hint defensively. "You are living together."

"We share a house," she said, rubbing her temple. "Not a room."

"All right, well, that's just fine," Allen said, sounding relieved. "Your rooms will be ready. Your mother is planning to make pecan cinnamon rolls for breakfast. Do Spencer or his brother have any allergies we should know about as we plan the rest of the meals?"

"No," Cassandra said awkwardly, unaccustomed to her family being so accommodating. "They'll eat pretty much anything."

"Excellent. We'll text you once we make a dinner plan, and you can let us know if there are any changes you'd like us to make. Do they like coffee?"

"Yes."

"Do they use creamer? We only have half and half."

"That's fine, Dad."

"All right. Let me know if there's anything you three need, and we'll make sure to have it."

"Thanks. I'll, uh—I'll see you Thursday."

"Sounds good, sweetheart. We look forward to it."

"Right. Goodbye."

"I love you."

Cassandra bit her lip, knowing he meant it in his own screwed-up way. "I love you too," she murmured guiltily, knowing she *didn't* mean it.

Returning to the kitchen, Cassandra found Spencer putting the first batch of gingerbread men into the oven while Peter worked on the chocolate chip cookies and Connor finished off the icing. She took a seat at the island and informed the men of the call, asking whether they were okay with the plan.

Peter turned to Connor. "You okay being here alone, Zeus?"

Connor shrugged casually. "Yeah, it's no big deal. I'll see if Aaron wants to hang out if I get bored."

"Cool." Peter cracked another egg and dropped it into the mixer. "Sounds good to me. Spence?"

At her side, Spencer smiled at Cassandra. "I'm game," he said. "I look forward to meeting them."

Cassandra almost melted like a chocolate chip in the oven under his tender gaze. "Try to remember you said that when we get there," she replied. Though somehow she thought that if there was anyone who could make the most out of their time with the Clements, it would be this wonderful man standing at her side.

CHAPTER SEVEN

Connor

After a long day of baking and decorating, Connor rode to The Glass Tavern with Spencer and Cassandra. Peter had left hours before for his shift—borrowing Cassandra's truck—and that was the moment that Connor first began to feel panic set in. With all the other activities in their day, he'd managed to ignore the fact that the Lamberts would arrive in town.

But when Peter had left them to finish up the last of the cookies (which had numbered around two hundred fifty on his last counting), a low dread writhed in Connor's gut.

Peter's encouragement at the grocery store did little good. Connor's personal experience of Andrew and Aimee's loving nature couldn't ease his worries. Not when he didn't deserve their goodness and mercy. Not after everything he'd done to their family.

Spencer drove the Jeep down the plowed curve of Whitehill Way and pulled onto Trinity Lane. The winding road led them past the upper neighborhoods of DeVerre, the funeral home, the chapel, and the fire station. All of it was covered in white, a gentle snowfall drifting from the sky to freshen the Earth's winter coat.

A few other vehicles lined the plaza's square, the Christmas tree shining brightly beside the town hall. A smattering of townspeople ambled along the sidewalks, though he knew most of the shopping would be done at the general store or in Spokane. Few DeVerreans bought their gifts in town these days. Whatever they needed, they ordered, traveled to purchase, or made themselves.

Spencer parallel parked behind Haley's white sedan. Cassandra's detail parked behind them, the men remaining in their vehicle to watch the perimeter. Connor tried not to tense when he stepped onto the salted sidewalk, seeing Ava's hatchback near the front. If the Bernards were here, so were the Lambert parents, as the couple would be staying with their eldest daughter.

Connor swallowed down his nerves and followed Spencer and Cassandra along the sidewalk. His feet stuttered when he saw the Kelly green awning, weighted down by snow, and the gold and green lettered windows coated in frost. He hadn't been in the tavern since Anna's death. He couldn't fathom entering its four walls, knowing she wasn't there. It wouldn't be right. It couldn't be.

The bell chimed as Spencer opened the door for Cassandra. He looked back, waiting for Connor to enter too.

Sucking in a sharp breath, Connor moved inside. Immediately, he saw Andrew and Aimee standing with their surviving children, unwinding scarves and removing coats near the bar. Peter was off serving a table; Sam Chapelle and his wife, Melanie, were in for one of their regular date nights. Spencer and Cassandra readily walked up to the Lambert family.

With caution, Connor approached too. Ava was introducing Spencer and Cassandra to Andrew and Aimee. The older couple gave them friendly smiles. Connor had always thought Anna looked the most like her mother out of all their children. They both shared rounder, softer features and bright smiles that overtook their faces. Both the Lambert daughters had inherited Aimee's sharp brow and high cheekbones. Her cedar-brown skin was deeper than any of her children, and she kept her dark brown hair straightened to hang in a crop just above her shoulders.

Andrew Lambert nearly towered over his wife, though he was slightly shorter than Connor. Ava looked most like her father, though Aaron shared his large forehead and deep-set, hooded eyes. Pale-complected and blue-eyed with light brown hair, he stuck out in his family. As the only non-native DeVerrean, he carried a subtle Canadian accent, just like Owen.

In fact, many things about Andrew and Aimee were like Owen and Ava. Both couples had met in college, and both husbands were the steady, gentle voice next to their bold and determined wives. Connor remembered when Ava had first brought Owen home from Spokane. The pair had only been dating a month, but they'd all known: If Ava was bringing a guy home, she was going to marry him. And it still stuck with Connor, the way Andrew and Aimee had immediately accepted Owen as a member of the family, just as they'd done with Haley.

Something Connor had hoped they would do with him.

A tremble worked through Connor's hands as he came to a stop at the back of the group. Aaron saw him first, giving him a chin-up in greeting. Connor returned the gesture. Which, unfortunately, caught Aimee's attention.

Connor stiffened as their eyes met. There was a stiltedness and a hesitation in her gaze. But Connor didn't see the hate he expected. No, he saw something far, far worse.

Hurt. Pain. Sorrow.

All the feelings he and his family had caused.

The rest of the group noticed Aimee's distraction, turning to face Connor too. His heart clenched, and he fought the urge to run.

Holding his ground, Connor opened his mouth. But instead of saying "hello" like any normal person should, he greeted Anna's parents with an immediate, "I'm sorry."

Aimee's brows drew together while Andrew gave Connor a flat, almost dumbfounded look.

An awkward moment of silence passed before Andrew sighed. At the far side of the group, he offered a pained smile. "It's good to see you again, Connor," he said.

Certain that this kind, if stilted, exchange was for Anna's sake, Connor bit his tongue. It would be easier on them if they could forget he was here. While they granted him the grace of not spewing hateful comments as they should, he would repay their kindness with his silence.

"Why don't we all take a seat?" Owen said, breaking the tense moment.

After a short shuffle, Connor found himself with the choice of sitting by Aaron, at the head of the table, or in the chair across from Aimee. Feeling that choice was no choice at all, Connor sat by Aaron.

With a final word to Ava at his side, Andrew turned to face Cassandra. "You're Allen Clement's daughter, right?" he asked.

"I am," she said, her shoulders drawing back.

Andrew nodded. "I remember Al. We were on the same softball team for a while. The Ravens. Then your family moved to Spokane, I believe."

"That's correct." Cassandra's fingers brushed the pinky finger of her right hand where she used to wear the Sauveterre ring. "They're still there."

"Wasn't he from Seattle originally?"

"Mirrormont, actually, but yes, it's basically Seattle."

Connor turned away from the conversation to see Aimee squeeze Haley's hand as she examined her engagement ring. "We'd like the ceremony to be at the chapel," Haley was saying. "But my parents offered their lodge for the reception."

"Oh, that will be beautiful," Aimee replied. "No matter the season, that view is stunning. Have you chosen a theme or are you just going for specific colors?"

"Blue," Aaron said decidedly.

Haley reached over to tap the bridge of his glasses. "Aaron had one request," she teased. "And that's blue because . . ."

At her prompting, Aaron immediately said, "It matches your eyes."

Feeling like an interloper, Connor turned away again. He shouldn't be part of this. Not after the way he'd betrayed them.

"Mkay," Peter said, suddenly showing up with a massive tray filled with drinks. He settled it on the table and began handing them out. "Technically, I'm still on duty, so if anyone needs me, you'll have to excuse me, but I think I'll be free for a bit. Andrew, here's that rye and ginger. You've got good taste."

Andrew accepted the cocktail with a curious grin, surely amused by Peter's gregarious nature.

"The house white for Mama Lambert."

Aimee wore an equally quizzical expression.

"Ava." Peter set a short glass in front of her, and Ava replied, "Peter."

He winked, gesturing to the drink. "Cherry fizz mocktail, just for you." Then he slid a highball glass filled with pink fizzy liquid and a sprig of some green herb. "The Bubbly-Blonde Signature made specially for Mrs. Lambert-to-Be."

Haley giggled as she accepted the personalized cocktail.

"A Pete Collins for Aaron. Unoriginal, man."

"It's really good," Aaron defended.

"Yeah, I'm aware." Peter grinned despite his sour tone. Then he set a coupe glass in front of Cassandra. "The Nyct for Cass."

She rolled her eyes but took an immediate sip of the purple gin and tonic anyway.

"Two wheat beers for our most boring patrons," Peter lamented, sliding the pints to Owen and Spencer. "And finally . . ."

Peter settled the last drink in front of Connor. In a rocks-style glass, yellow liquid rippled around the ice, a peel of lemon skewered on a toothpick, and a sprig of what he thought was rosemary on top.

"What's this?" Connor asked.

"I call it—" Peter drew his hand through the air dramatically, "The Golden God. It's got Bourbon, lemon juice, and a splash of tonic to lighten it up. The rosemary is just for looks, to represent the Greek laurels."

At Connor's annoyed look, Peter pointed at him. "Try it before you send it back," he ordered.

"You've made signature cocktails for everyone?" Aimee asked, something between bafflement and amusement in her tone.

Peter looked over at her with a smile. "Yeah," he said, as though that's what everyone did. "Though Spence won't let me make him one."

"I'm not a liquor person," Spencer defended.

Neither was Connor, but he didn't speak up for fear of drawing attention to himself.

"Anyway," Peter said, taking the remaining empty seat between Connor and Cassandra. "We're happy to meet you both finally. And we welcome whatever questions you have."

Andrew and Aimee shared a meaningful look before turning back to Peter.

"Our children have explained the past month to us," Aimee said without preamble. "About the spirit world, Wielders, the Warden, Druids, and . . . everything else."

Connor's gaze drifted toward Peter, Spencer, and Cassandra. The three exchanged glances, the men flanking Cassandra as protective guards. That "everything else" surely encompassed her new role as the presumed Vessel for the final Spectral—the Ancient One, as the Druids called her. That wasn't general knowledge around the town. Still, the Lambert/Bernard family had quickly become predominant figures in the DeVerrean Warden, if only because of their role in protecting the town at the Varon brothers' side.

"What they couldn't tell us," Aimee continued, "was what you, your brother, and Miss Clement intend to do now that you're the most influential people in DeVerre."

Spencer raised his brow while Peter shifted uncomfortably. Cassandra, however, kept her head held high. "We intend to protect it," she said.

"Wonderful," Andrew said with a thread of good-natured sarcasm. "How?"

At Connor's side, Peter glanced out toward the rest of the tavern. Only Sam and Melanie Chapelle ate at a far booth. Both trustworthy, though not as aware as the inner circle of Cassandra's detail and the primary Warden leadership within DeVerre.

Peter cleared his throat. "We can't be as open as we'd like in a more public location," he said, fingering his golden ring. "But as Varons, Spencer and I plan on helping bring back order within DeVerre . . . With or without the Warden's approval."

"Which," Spencer added, "looks like safeguarding the Veil, defending the town, and ensuring that the Druids won't ever get a foothold here again. By whatever means necessary."

"But what is your specific plan?" Aimee pressed. "The last Varons were killed, and the Druids managed to manipulate the entire town through their lies. They created a whole narrative, suppressing the truth and destroying all information to refute their claims."

Connor quelled the urge to slump in his seat. That was his family she was talking about. While there were other Druids in DeVerre, the Frossards were the leaders from the start. They'd made their way into Harmony generations before Matthias Varon ever founded DeVerre. Then they'd solidified their place amongst the elite of the town, making sure that they could twist the truth over the generations. It was Connor's generation that was supposed to inherit the town and control of the Spectral with it.

Out of the corner of his eye, Conor caught Ava staring at him as though she knew his thoughts. He averted his gaze, fingers chilled on the cocktail glass before him.

"Well . . ." Peter began. "It's hard to say for sure. I mean, we don't know what the future holds, so we'll have to change course as things come, but . . . For now, our specific plan is to train, to grow stronger—as Wielders and as individuals—and to work with the Warden to get the town back to a safe place."

Spencer nodded as Cassandra jumped in. "While we eradicated the Druids, we also lost many of the important people within DeVerre in their ranks," she said. "Those are roles that have to be filled. And while the Warden has brought many people in to help with that, we need to make sure that they aren't just here to do as the Warden says. We want to know that they truly care about the town. Because this is our home, even if I was gone for twenty years and Peter and Spencer only moved here two months ago."

"Exactly," Spencer agreed. "We're working with Jeremiah Rhader, Helen Dryer, and Owen—" He gestured to the man at his side, "to make sure that every position filled in the town is taken by people who will add to the community rather than simply fill a role."

"And, of course," Peter added, clapping Connor on the shoulder, "Zeus here will be taking his place as the town doctor just as soon as he graduates."

Swallowing his anxiety, Connor kept his eyes downcast as he clarified, "I still have a few years of residency to complete, so I'll do that under Doctor Bell, who's taken the job temporarily."

A silent moment passed as the Lamberts took all of this in. Connor wondered if they were questioning the wisdom of accepting him as a vital member of the township. Perhaps they thought it'd be better for him to be left out of the situation entirely.

Instead of voicing this concern, Andrew asked, "Those people you mentioned—Jeremy Rhader and Helen Dryer?"

"Jeremiah," Spencer corrected. "Rhader is the head of Sheraton Corporation's Municipality Supervision Department, specializing in the direction of towns which house . . ." He glanced at Cassandra. "Veils."

"And Helen is a Relationship Ambassador," Peter explained. "It's her job to make sure DeVerre's transition to a Warden-run government goes smoothly with the citizens' best interests in mind."

Aimee and Andrew took in this information with thoughtful faces. Andrew sipped his cocktail while Aimee folded her hands on the tabletop. She glanced over at Ava, who gave her a firm nod.

With a determined glimmer in her eyes, Aimee turned back to the four across from her. "And how exactly do you plan to bring our daughter back?" she asked, but the question wasn't directed at Peter, Cassandra, or Spencer. She spoke with her gaze locked on Connor.

Shocked at being addressed, Connor's lips parted, but no words found their way out.

"We're not totally sure," Peter said quietly, saving him. "Connor and I have been doing a lot of studying. Resurrection is a touchy subject amongst the Warden, and since Connor's not a Druid anymore, he can't reach out to anyone who might actually have the answers there. Not that we're sure many of them know either."

"It was in the codex," Connor said, finding his voice at last. "I'm sure of that. But it was taken before I could get to it."

"I do have a question," Andrew said. "The spirit world operates under God's authority, right?"

When everyone turned to Owen as the resident expert on the subject, he said, "Yes."

Andrew's expression pinched. "Then how is it that Druids can resurrect people the same as Christians? Evil shouldn't have control over such things, should it?"

"The whole subject is theoretical," Owen said hesitantly. "I've never actually witnessed resurrection in all my years with the Warden. There are rumors, of course, but nothing that I've been able to confirm. But there are many instances in the Bible of even those in opposition to God working miracles. The magicians of Pharaoh. Seers and witches. The Druids can wield the power of the spirit world, just like us. It's just that their powers are tainted by cruelty and greed. God won't stop a miracle from occurring, even by corrupted hands. He allows His glory to be displayed, however it might manifest."

Andrew sat back, considering.

In the ensuing quiet, Connor leaned forward. "This is different than Biblical resurrection, though," he said. "That is viable and exclusively determined by God's power moving through His people. This is connected to the spirit world and wielding. Only Wielders can become ghosts, and only ghosts can be tethered—to a location, as a phantom . . . or to their body, as a resurrected being."

"How do you know this?" Owen asked.

Connor paused, uncomfortable with the entire table staring at him. "It's what my dad told me. He was never planning to follow through with his promise to Gerard because—well, his and Franklin's bodies didn't exist anymore. They've been dead for almost seventy years. There's nothing but bones to tether to, and that's not enough."

Cassandra's jaw tensed, and several of the others shifted uneasily at the thought.

Seeing the need to impress the truth upon them, Connor kept going. "The Warden claims this is theoretical," he said. "But I know it isn't. The Druids have accomplished resurrection, though not widely. It's difficult, it's demanding, but it *is* possible."

"But you don't know how to do it," Aimee said, not like an accusation but as a matter of fact.

"Not yet," Connor admitted. "But we're getting close."

"The first thing," Peter jumped in, "is finding Anna's ghost. Which we're struggling to do."

"And if she didn't become a ghost . . . ?" Aimee asked.

"She did," Connor said determinedly.

"How do you know? You said only Wielders could become ghosts. As far as I was aware, she wasn't one."

While Connor didn't know for sure whether or not Anna had become a Wielder, though he had no actual evidence, he said, "She's not gone."

Ava sat forward, lending her firm voice to the conversation. "Once we find her," she said steadily, "we will tether her back to her body, which is currently being kept at the morgue under Gabe's watch."

Andrew frowned. "I thought the town believed she was in Canada."

"They do. Outside of our group, only Gabe, his niece, and Haley's brothers know about her death. And none of them will tell anyone."

Andrew and Aimee didn't seem convinced but accepted their words all the same.

A thread of hope filled Connor's chest. With Ava's confidence and Peter's strange ability to gain people's trust, it seemed that the Lamberts were giving them their faith. But Connor needed to make sure they knew how seriously he took this mission. Even if they never forgave him, they needed to know that he would stop at nothing to right his wrongs—to bring Anna back.

"One last thing," Connor interjected. "From my research, there needs to be a sacrifice made to bring someone back. I'm not entirely certain what that looks like yet, but I want you to know: *whatever* it is, I'll make it."

Andrew and Aimee stared at him.

He drew back his shoulders, resolute. "Even if it's my own life."

Worry creased Andrew's brow while Aimee narrowed her gaze.

Connor didn't care if they doubted him. He would give everything for Anna's sake. It wasn't to redeem himself or to prove his goodness. It was because he loved her, and if anyone deserved to live, it was Anna Lambert.

A long, painful silence hung in the air. During which time, Sam raised his hand at the far side of the tavern, signaling for Peter's assistance. Peter excused himself to cash them out, breaking the awkward moment.

Aaron leaned on the table, the drink before him empty. "So," he prompted, "you got what you needed?"

The Lambert parents shared another of their significant looks. Then Andrew smiled in that soft manner of his. "I think we have," he said and turned to Spencer. "You and your brother are interesting people. I see now why my children all believe in you so strongly. I have the urge to do the same. Though, admittedly, I don't fully understand why."

"It's a Varon trait," Aimee remarked dryly. "According to my family's records, at least."

Several light chuckles were passed around the table.

Somehow, in half an hour, Peter and Spencer had gained the Lambert parents' support. Connor wondered how the brothers managed to achieve such loyalty. What was it about them that inspired people to want to follow their lead? It wasn't simply that they were Varons, was it? Could a family lineage really be so strong as to grant its bloodline automatic leadership?

He didn't know, but somehow, he, too, was willing to give Peter and Spencer his loyalty. Not just because Anna would. Because he believed in them and their goodness. He believed they wanted the best for each other, for the people they loved, and for the town around them.

Maybe that's why they were so easy to follow. They were guileless. And after an entire lifetime being raised by a father and mother who lived by the rule of duplicity, Connor could use some simple honesty.

Watching as the Lamberts and Bernards rose, Connor wondered if they'd ever come to trust him with that same ready loyalty. Could he redeem himself in their eyes? Would whatever sacrifices he made to save their daughter regain their trust? Or would he be destined to remain on the outside of their family?

After everything he'd done, Connor rather hoped Anna's resurrection cost him his life. Then, he'd never have to find out.

CHAPTER EIGHT

Peter

The sun reflected off the snow drifts with blinding precision. Peter squinted, cresting the hill that overlooked DeVerre Lake. After talking with the Lamberts the night before, he couldn't shake the need to find Anna. Immediately.

He and Connor had worked so long and so hard. It just didn't sit right with him, the fact that they hadn't found her ghost yet. And after what Connor had said last night . . .

Peter could admit that he was worried. Last he'd known, Anna hadn't been a Wielder. That would mean that she hadn't become a ghost. And that would end all their hope of bringing her back.

But then, he'd thought he wasn't a Wielder, and then he'd summoned forth that burst of golden light that saved Anna's life. What if she had been a Wielder and hadn't known it? After all, she'd experienced dozens of supernatural experiences over the final weeks of her life.

The thought sent a cold shiver through his veins.

Back at the lake, Peter walked along its edge. A gentle mist drifted off the icy surface. He tromped through the trees, seeing the occasional gray shimmer of a ghost. Frossards, Sauveterres, Alaries. He even thought he saw Gerard for a moment, though the once-phantom disappeared into the forest too quickly for him even to consider approaching.

After an hour of wandering, Peter returned to the lakeside. His limbs were numb, and his cheeks burned from the cold. His heart felt frosted over, devoid of hope, as he stared unseeingly across the expanse of the frozen water.

Shaking off the thought, Peter reminded himself that this was why they were celebrating. Life was heavy. Christmas was light. He couldn't remove the pain and weight of responsibility in their lives. But he *could* make sure they all found the momentary rest they needed. He could take care of his loved ones, even if he'd failed Anna.

Peter ran a hand over his mouth, the cold band of the Varon ring brushing his lips. He couldn't wear gloves with the thing. It always felt wrong.

With a forced out breath, Peter shoved his hand back into his pocket and scanned the tree line across from him.

"Hey, Annie," he said to the cold winter air. "Merry Christmas."

The silence of winter was his only reply. This wasn't the first time he'd spoken to the non-existent presence of Anna. But this time, it felt more important than the others.

"I'm sorry that we haven't found you yet. We really are trying, and if you're out here . . . we'll find you, and then we'll bring you back."

Nothing.

Peter sighed. "Your parents are here. I met them last night." A wry grin pulled at his lips. "They're pretty cool, but that's to be expected, I guess, seeing as their kids are pretty great too. They're trusting us, and that's . . ."

He didn't know how to finish that sentence. The Lambert parents' trust was encouraging, demanding, wonderful, and overwhelming. He couldn't decide whether it made him feel hopeful or more at a loss. What if he failed them? What if he and Connor were wrong? If Anna wasn't out here, they'd be wasting the whole of the Lambert family's time. They'd be prolonging their grieving, only to let them down.

Peter thought of Anna's body, locked in one of those storage drawers in Gabe Chapelle's morgue. He'd never gone to visit her there. It didn't make sense to him. She wasn't in her body. She was either a ghost out here by the lake, or she was gone. And he didn't care to see her broken body until he knew he could restore her spirit to it.

Throat going dry, Peter whispered to the wind, "The town feels empty without you, Anne. I don't know if you know this, but you were kind of the heart of DeVerre. You made it worth living in. And now that you're gone . . ."

He sucked in his bottom lip against the rising emotion in his chest. "Anyway," he sighed. "We've got to get you back, that's that. So, maybe show up sometime soon, okay? We miss you."

The forest was still, not a sign of life among the trees. No woodland creatures. No birds. Not even a ghost. It was as though DeVerre itself was warning him, telling him to manage his expectations.

"Right."

Peter turned away from the lake and headed back up the hill. He scrambled up the slope, fighting the thick snowbanks and icy roots. A cool breeze whipped through as he made his way home. The pines towered above him, every inch of the forest known to him now. He'd hiked it almost daily over the last month. He'd run through it in his nightmares from the valravn. And just last night, he'd found himself dreaming of it again.

It wasn't the first time since his captivity that his dreams returned to the raven, to the woman.

Peter saw the hollow from a distance, dropping his gaze to his boots. He always told himself he'd take a different route to the lake next time. There was no reason to walk past this stand of trees, no reason to torture himself with more questions he didn't have answers to. Like, why had this dream lingered while all the others from the valravn had disappeared when Connor sent the beast back to the spirit world? Why did the raven come to him? And who was the woman with it?

Fisting his hands in his pockets, Peter told himself to keep moving. He shouldn't feel any attachment to this particular spot. It wasn't important, it wasn't special. It was just a strange recurring dream that didn't mean anything.

As if on their own accord, Peter's feet came to a gradual stop. He still faced Occasus, the hollow to his right. He gritted his teeth, the dream replaying in his mind.

He wasn't running anymore in the dreams. The cries for help from his family had disappeared too. In fact, the whole experience was rather serene. Now, Peter was simply walking, coming around the bend to see the moonlight and the mist. The raven flew in, gliding through the air with its shimmering blue-black wings. The thick fog would part, drawing back in coils to reveal *her*.

Peter's breath caught every time. With hope, with awe, with anticipation. The silver light of the moon lit her up, her head tipped back to stare at its full face. The wind teased her red hair, its long curls loose and wispy. Her navy coat fluttered around her calves, hands tucked into their pockets.

The raven would land on her shoulder, crooning softly to her. Forest Lady, as he called her, would turn then, her profile silhouetted in the night.

In the bright light of day, Peter found himself staring at the hollow, remembering the dream. It started snowing; the flecks gently floated onto his head and the pines around him. Even in the daylight, the hollow glowed with an almost ethereal reality. He expected the raven to flutter into view at any second, its midnight-blue-black wings a stark contrast to the white cascade of snow around him. He could imagine the trim, lithe figure of Forest Lady standing there, her rose-gold hair freckled with snow, like pearls woven into its strands.

But there was nothing there.

"I don't know if you're real," Peter told the empty forest. "But if you are . . . It'd be nice to meet you soon."

The forest was silent, a sun flare cutting through the clouds.

Peter scoffed at himself. "Take your time, though," he said with a derisive smile. "I'll be ready whenever."

Then, he continued on his way to Occasus, leaving behind all thoughts of the woman and the raven.

~

When Peter returned to Occasus, he found Cassandra in the living room working on her ornament while Spencer sat in the office. He took a seat across from Spencer, seeing what he was up to. They talked about *Wenzel & Frankly*, then Peter caught the way Spencer spaced out for a moment, staring at Cassandra.

"How are you doin'?" Peter asked quietly. "About meeting Cass's family, I mean. You nervous or anything?"

"Kind of," Spencer admitted. "I don't want to screw it up, but, honestly, I'm just concerned about being there for Cass."

"I said it from the start," Peter teased. "You'll make a great wife someday."

"Shut up."

He smiled encouragingly at his brother. "If you need anything while we're there, just let me know."

"Thanks." Spencer paused, then asked, "How are you doing?"

Peter furrowed his brow. "With what?"

Spencer just stared at him knowingly.

Swallowing, Peter shrugged nonchalantly. "I'm getting there. There's just . . . a lot to figure out."

"With Anna? Or with being the true Varon?"

"The Varon bit hasn't come up much."

"That doesn't change the fact that you're a leader now."

Peter gave a wry grin. "Can you be a leader when you don't have anyone or anything to lead?"

"Don't do that to yourself."

"Do what?"

"Don't lie to yourself to make you feel less important than you are." Spencer held his gaze determinedly. "You're a leader, Pete. Whether you feel like it or not, you lead Cass, Connor, and me every day. We look to you."

Peter blinked in surprise.

"This town looks to you."

Peter didn't know how to reply to that. Was it true? Did he have any place among the leadership of DeVerre? He didn't feel like it. In all their meetings and talks, he always felt like a kid attempting to appear like one of the adults.

"I'm done," Cassandra announced, interrupting Peter's thoughts.

The brothers went into the living room to see her work. She hung the star-shaped ornament on the tree. Made of red and white felt haphazardly stitched together and with a button hot-glued in the center, it was probably the simplest and most poorly made of all their handmade ornaments that year.

But Spencer had insisted she make it, and Peter knew he wanted her to feel she'd done well, so they both lied.

"It looks great," Spencer insisted.

Cassandra sent him a scathing glare. "Really? What about it is 'great'?"

"I like the button. It was a nice touch."

"I seriously hate crafts," Cassandra said, glaring at the uneven star she'd made.

"I don't see what's wrong with it," Peter said, gesturing to the tree. "It's . . . great. And it looks perfect with Diane's stuff."

"Don't patronize me."

"I'm not."

Her brow arched knowingly.

Peter rolled his eyes. "If you're determined to think the worst of your skills, that's on you."

Spencer chuckled at the flat look Cassandra was giving Peter. "I'll be right back," he said. "I've got to finish uploading the episode, then we'll be officially done with *Wenzel & Frankly* for the year."

As Spencer headed toward the office, Peter surveyed the felt star again. "You know, it is rather simple, but I think that's part of its charm."

Cassandra crossed her arms with a "humph."

Nudging her side, Peter lowered his voice and met her gaze. "Not that I'm an expert in the ways of romance, but your boyfriend values this tradition, so you might want to practice your crafting skills."

Pursing her lips, Cassandra sent a scathing look at the tree. "This tradition sucks," she grumbled.

Peter chuckled, then turned to the office where Spencer was uploading the *Wenzel & Frankly* Christmas Special to their blog. Spencer clicked a couple of times on the trackpad, then pushed back from the desk. "Done," he said with a smile. "The Special is officially scheduled to release on Christmas Eve, and then our readers will know they have a whole book to look forward to next year."

"Great!" Peter rubbed his hands together excitedly. "Ready to play Santa and deliver these cookies?"

Spencer and Cassandra shared a lackluster look. "I guess," he said.

"Oh, come on," Peter said with disappointment. "Christmas is about giving, especially to those who are going without. And while these kids may not be gift-less this year—Helen mentioned something about a toy drive—they lost their parents. They could use some holiday cheer."

"And it helps foster their goodwill," Cassandra added cynically.

Peter frowned. "That's *not* why I want to do this."

She waved him off. "Let's just get the tins and get this over with."

"You people are the personification of Christmas cheer," he snarked, then waved off their poor attitudes. "Either of you know what Connor's up to?"

"Not sure," Spencer said. "I think he's in his room."

"Right." Peter moved away from the office. "I'll get him."

After taking the front staircase two steps at a time, Peter moved through the hall and back to the guest room where Connor stayed when he was in DeVerre. Though he'd likely hidden up here to avoid joining the cookie-gifting excursion, Peter knocked on the door. They all needed to remember the purpose of Christmas. And what better way to do that than by giving to hurting children?

At Connor's beckoning call, Peter opened the door. "You ready, man?" he asked.

Connor lay back on the bed, a book in his hands. He glanced over the top. "For what?" he replied, though he knew very well what. They'd made their plans just this morning at breakfast.

"Cookies, dude," Peter said.

Connor raised his book once more. "I'll pass."

"That's not an option."

With an annoyed sigh, Connor gave him a flat stare. "You do realize that I'm the reason these kids lost their parents, don't you?" he said. "Any of them who *don't* blame me are either too young to understand or stupid enough to believe that I'm playing some long game to restore the Druids to the town."

Peter tightened his jaw, not bothering to remind him that every single one of these kids *knew* that he, Spencer, and Cassandra were responsible for their parents' deaths. But that was the point. Like Connor, these kids had been raised by cultists. These kids needed to understand that their parents, loving or not, were in the wrong, just as Connor had determined about his own dad and mom. And the only way to do that was to show them that they—as the Varons and part of the Warden—weren't the bad guys.

"It's the right thing to do," Peter said.

"Then you do it."

Peter rolled his eyes. "You're such a grump," he muttered.

"I'm a realist."

"How'd you and Anna ever get along?"

Peter had said it as a joke, but Connor tensed. "It was different," he said defensively. "With her . . . I was different."

"Nice?" Peter prompted.

"Hopeful."

Peter pressed his lips together, feeling somewhat like a jerk for bringing up the sore subject.

Shaking his head, Connor motioned to the book. "Once I figure out how to save her," he said pointedly, "*then* I'll help you deliver cookies."

The obvious answer was on the tip of Peter's tongue. There was no doubt in his mind that Anna would tell Connor to join them, hand out tins of cookies, and help dozens of hurting kids find a fraction of joy in this holiday season. But after his dejected walk through the forest earlier, Peter was in a unique position to understand what Connor was going through.

Tapping the doorframe, Peter backed up. "All right," he said. "Let me know what you find. And if you change your mind. . . ."

He let the words hang, shutting the door behind him as he left.

Peter nudged his Varon ring as he returned to the stairs. Was this what being a leader meant? Knowing when to let people wallow and when to tell them to pick themselves up, dust themselves off, and try again? If so, he worried he wouldn't be very good at that. Even now, he felt like a failure, unsure of what Connor really needed in this moment. Was it best for him to stay behind to study? Or would it do him more good to be out in the world, experiencing the true meaning of Christmas?

Just as Peter set his first foot on the top stair, he heard a door open behind him. He turned to see Connor emerge, a sour look on his face.

Peter raised his brow in surprise.

"Shut up," Connor said.

"I didn't say anything."

"It's what Anna would want," Connor grumbled, joining him on the stairs.

CHAPTER NINE

Connor

With the cookies doled out into decorative tins, the group piled into the Jeep and headed out into DeVerre. Behind them, Cassandra's detail was extra watchful due to the purpose of this cookie mission. Peter had a list (in his notebook, of course) of each residence they needed to visit. Fifteen households in total. Thirty-two children. However, only ten of those had lost both parents to the fight at the Veil.

Connor knew that several of the older children—mostly thirteen or above—considered themselves to be Druids. So when Peter read off his list, Connor made sure to warn about the ones who would likely harbor the most anger toward their group.

It was a singularly miserable experience, going from house to house, seeing displaced children and mourning spouses. That was one of the things Connor disapproved of most; the Druids often encouraged their members to lie to their spouses, keeping them ignorant for the sake of the cause. He remembered one meeting where his father had said, *"The more we disseminate through the populace unseen, the more easily we control the town."*

Peter had asked Helen to call each household to ask if they'd be welcome in the first place. So many of the parents—whether surviving or adoptive—were quite welcoming when they arrived with their gifts. Others were standoffish, seemingly only accepting for the kids' sake.

Several of their stops were short, a mere greeting at the door to drop off the tins. But a few families offered for them to come inside and have a cup of cocoa or a cookie themselves as they greeted the kids.

Some children were excited by the cookies and chatted happily about what they hoped to get for Christmas with their visitors. Others were reluctant and nervous, accepting the cookies but not interested in a conversation. A few were openly hostile.

One, a sixteen-year-old named Carl, took the tin, opened it, and dumped the contents in the trash before turning to Connor to say, "They were counting on you. And you betrayed them."

Worse, Lindsey Frossard, his nine-year-old first cousin once removed, sidled up to him while the others were distracted by her five-year-old sister, Claire, to whisper, "I don't care what the others say. I still believe you're on our side."

Connor didn't have to ask what she meant. It was the same sentiment that had many of the Warden members keeping an eye on him when he was in town. They thought that Connor was a double agent, working to bring down the Varons by currying their favor.

This was why Connor didn't want to join this excursion. These horrible encounters and the knowledge that no matter what he did, nothing would prove that he'd changed. Not until he'd saved Anna.

But he knew that if Anna were here, she'd go, whether the kids hated her or not. So, Connor chose to honor her and her wonderful, loving nature.

Now, it felt like a mistake.

"All right," Peter said with a heavy sigh. "That was number eleven. So, we've only got four more to go."

"Only four, huh?" Cassandra said, her tone suggesting the same exhaustion Connor felt.

Peter grimaced. "I'll admit, this is harder than I thought it'd be."

"It's okay," Spencer said, keeping his eyes on the road as he drove down the street. "This was a good idea, and if nothing else, we've made several kids really happy."

"And others, really pissed," Connor offered, staring out the window. "Though to be fair, they deserved it."

"Their parents died," Cassandra said.

"And they consider themselves to be Druids," he returned. "Immaturity doesn't negate responsibility. Even my ass of a father knew that."

A thick silence fell in the car. Because what could they say? Druidic children were just as dangerous as their parents. In fact, they might be even more dangerous, holding a grudge against the Varon brothers and Cassandra. They were like ticking time bombs; if someone didn't defuse them, they were going to explode, hurting more than just themselves in the process.

And Connor wasn't about to watch them destroy his home in the name of their screwed-up parents.

Spencer pulled to a stop. "Which kid is this?" he asked.

Peter glanced at his notebook. "Josiah Frossard."

Connor flinched, staring at the house in the distance.

"He's six," Peter continued to read. "He lost both his parents, Adrian and Alyssa. Now, he lives with his aunt and uncle, Jermaine and Katherine Calderon, though they're just fostering him."

Peter turned to Connor. "Isn't this the kid the Warden—?"

"Yeah," Connor cut him off. "He's a nice kid. This'll be an easy stop."

"Good," Cassandra said wearily. "We could use one of those."

They got out, took the cookie tin from the box in the trunk, and then headed up the snowy lawn to the front door. As farmers, the Calderons lived on the outskirts of town. Their house was small, old, and likely in good need of repair, and to Connor's knowledge, Jermaine's mother lived with them, making the already cramped house even more packed. It was little wonder they didn't feel they could add another child to the chaos.

As they stepped onto the porch, Connor saw Jermaine and his cousin, Kyle, working on the fence where the cows grazed on the frosted grass. The sun was dimming, making the shadows lengthen in the early winter evening. Peter took the lead as he had all day, though Connor noticed how he had to draw in an intentional breath before he forced a smile on his face.

Katherine Calderon answered the door, her dirty blonde hair and striking features reminiscent of her Frossard ancestry. She'd lost two of her three brothers to the battle at the Veil. As the son of Alexander, Connor knew that it was her father who had been a Druid. Her mother had known nothing, and under Alexander's guidance, her father had chosen not to reveal the spirit world to his daughter or youngest son to keep the majority of the town ignorant.

"Merry Christmas," Peter said, holding out the cookie tin.

A hesitantly friendly smile came to Katherine's face as she took them in. "It's kind of you to do this," she said, then paused, her eyes flickering to Connor. "Would you like to come in? I know Siah would love to see you."

Connor grimaced internally. But after years of playing the role of the happy Frossard son, he managed to return her kind smile. "Of course," he said.

Katherine stepped back, letting them in. They didn't bother removing their coats, since they didn't intend to stay long. She led them to the living room, where two teen boys sat flanking a younger one on the couch, watching Batman cartoons. The six-year-old clutched two Matchbox cars to his chest, eyes wide as he watched the superhero zoom out of the Batcave in his Batmobile.

Connor's heart squeezed at the sight. He'd always liked Josiah Frossard. The kid was open, cheerful, and obsessed with cars of every type. Even after his parents' deaths, Josiah hadn't lost his spark, though he had become more wary of strangers and clung more tightly to those he knew and trusted.

"Boys," Katherine said. "We have company."

The minute Josiah saw Connor, he leaped off the couch and sailed across the room. The boy crashed into Connor's legs, wrapping his arms around his knees, Matchbox cars digging into his skin. "Conn-ur!" he exclaimed, his childish rhotacism still not able to quite pronounce the name right.

Setting a hand on the boy's fluffy blond head, Connor fought the urge to push him away. He found himself holding his breath as though enduring something impossibly painful. Josiah was a reminder of Connor's own childhood, believing so strongly in his parents and their goodness, only to learn they were wolves in sheep's clothing. And he didn't know how to handle that.

"We come bearing cookies," Peter said, coming near with the tin held out. "It's not quite frankincense or myrrh, but it'll do."

Josiah hid behind Connor, eyeing Peter skeptically.

"It's okay, Siah," Connor promised. "Pete's a friend."

"Mama said he's a heretic," Josiah whispered.

Connor pressed his lips together as Peter's brow raised.

"Your mama was wrong," Connor said firmly but kindly. He crouched down, though he still had to stoop to meet the boy's gaze. "Peter, Spencer, and Cassandra are our friends. They want to protect DeVerre *and* you."

Josiah stared up at Connor, blue eyes wide and begging for something to trust in. Connor could see the fear in him. The boy felt alone and abandoned by the parents who were taken from him. He needed something steady and true in his life. He needed *someone* to rely on.

Hardening himself to the guilt in his gut, Connor guided Josiah forward. "Take the cookies," he instructed.

Cautiously, Josiah did as ordered.

"Merry Christmas," Peter said as Spencer and Cassandra smiled softly behind him.

Josiah returned the greeting in a voice so muffled it could barely be heard.

Peter glanced up at Connor before addressing the kid again. "You've got a pretty cool cousin," he said.

That seemed to improve Josiah's opinion of the Varon. He blinked, a slight grin coming to his lips. "Yeah," he agreed. "Have you seen his Rover?"

Connor could see that it took Peter a second to realize the boy was talking about the Land Rover. Then, he smirked knowingly. "I've *ridden* in it."

Josiah's eyes went wide. "Really?" The word was a reverent hush.

"Yep." Peter pointed at Connor. "He saved my life, did you know that?"

Josiah shook his head, mouth agape in awe.

"I call him Zeus because he's basically a demigod."

"Zeus was a god," Spencer muttered. "Hercules was a demigod."

"Details," Peter said with a dismissive wave.

Unconcerned with the brothers' debate, Josiah looked up at Connor with even more wonder than usual.

Connor tried not to reveal his irritation. He patted Josiah's shoulder. "Why don't you go watch the rest of your show?" he suggested.

Josiah glanced toward the television, the cookie tin clutched awkwardly in his arms as he still clung to his metal toy cars. Then he shuffled closer to Connor and crooked a finger, beckoning him closer.

Connor knelt once again so that Josiah could whisper—or rather, speak at a normal volume, affecting his voice to sound as though he were *trying* to whisper. "Are you leaving again?" the boy asked.

"Uh . . ." Connor glanced over at Katherine for help.

The woman stepped up and reached for the cookie tin. "Here, Siah," she said. "Let me put this away. Jalen, Jason, come get a cookie."

The teen boys rushed after their mom, while Peter, Spencer, and Cassandra backed away, leaving Connor to talk with Josiah alone.

As this was the *opposite* of the help he'd been hoping for, Connor gritted his teeth only for a second before relaxing his jaw. "Listen," he said, then caught sight of the cars in Josiah's hands once again. He decided to change tactics. "Could I see one of those?"

Josiah readily handed one to him, and Connor stood, offering his hand to the boy. Tiny, cold fingers clung to his, and he led them to the race track at the back of the room. Connor set his car on the bright orange track and gave it a push. Josiah smiled, following his lead.

While they played with the cars, Connor cleared his throat. "Yeah, I gotta leave, Siah," he said, focusing on the shiny green lacquer of his hot rod rather than the boy beside him. "I've got to finish up medical school."

"How long does that take?"

"Only a few more months. I graduate in May."

"That's a long time."

"Not really." Connor set his car expertly careening around the loop-de-loop.

Josiah laughed in glee. "Mine always falls," he said, attempting it with his cherry red Mustang as though to prove his point.

At the crest of the ramp, the convertible dropped to the ground.

"You've just got to give it enough force," Connor instructed.

"What's force?"

"How hard you push it."

Josiah shoved his car forward on the track, but it tumbled off the ramp wildly.

Connor smiled dryly. "It takes practice," he said. "If you don't push strongly enough, it won't have enough force to make it around the loop. If you push too hard, the force will send it out of control."

Josiah tipped his head, trying again. It didn't work, but he wasn't deterred. "Will you come back after school?" he asked as he practiced.

"Yeah."

Josiah looked up at him. "Will you stay then?"

Connor hesitated, knowing that the boy wanted more from him than he could give. "Yeah," he repeated, then added, "But you may not see me as much as you used to."

The boy frowned. "Why not?"

"Things are different now," he said. "And I've got new responsibilities."

"Because you have to take Uncle Alex's job?"

"No," Connor said, maybe too aggressively. Though Alexander wasn't really Josiah's uncle, all the Frossard children called him that. As though he were some benevolent father figure.

Connor cleared his throat and began again. "No, no one's taking his job. Uncle Alex—my dad . . . He wasn't a good man, Josiah. And I don't want to be like him."

Josiah pursed his lips, clearly not understanding. He ran his car over the track aimlessly. "Who do you want to be like?" he asked quietly.

"Anna," Connor said without hesitation.

Josiah's mouth quirked to the side. "I miss Anna. When is she coming back?"

"Soon."

"Good." Josiah tried the ramp again, but his Mustang flipped off the track. Then he looked up at Connor with determined blue eyes. "I want to be like you."

Connor wanted to tell him no. No one should be like him. But he saw it in the little boy's adamant gaze: he *needed* someone to look up to.

Feeling dreadfully inadequate, Connor gave a weak smile. "I've gotta go," he said, then stood.

Josiah leaped up next to him. "Here," he said, holding out the red Mustang.

Connor stared at it. "What?"

"Take it."

"Why?"

"You brought me cookies for Christmas," Josiah said. "I'm giving you my car."

Sure that the boy would be dreadfully upset that he'd given away his favorite toy the second it was gone, Connor began to reject it. But something stopped him. He might not be able to give the boy the family he wished for, but he could make him happy, knowing that Connor would never forget about him with this little car in his possession.

Reaching out, Connor took the tiny, cherry red Mustang. "Thanks," he said.

Josiah smiled. "Next time you visit," he said proudly, "I'll be able to do the loop."

Connor ruffled the boy's hair. "Sounds good," he said with a chuckle.

But Connor knew he wasn't going to come back. He couldn't be a role model for this boy. He couldn't be an example for anyone. He wasn't even sure what goodness was at this point. How could he ever hope to teach someone what was right?

He wanted to be like Anna, but he knew that no matter how hard he worked, he would never be that good. His past irrevocably broke him. And the only way he could be of use to anyone was if he had her. That's why he *had* to bring her back.

Connor clutched the Mustang more tightly in his hand as he stepped onto the porch. If he was going to prove his goodness, he had to have Anna at his side. Otherwise, he'd just be a Druid masquerading as a hero. Without her to guide him, he was nothing but a ghost.

CHAPTER TEN

Cassandra

Cassandra couldn't believe that she'd agreed to this meeting. After the long day she'd had, delivering cookies with Spencer, Peter, and Connor, she was in no mood for this conversation.

She stepped into the coffee shop anyway, tugging off her scarf. The evening light shone golden through the window. Her ex, Jacob Howser, already sat at a table, away from the only other patrons—a Warden member talking to cousins Juliet and Malachi Chapelle, who were determined to become Sage Wielders to help in the restoration of DeVerre.

Jacob gave a gentle wave as Cassandra entered. He was as sophisticated as ever, his hair carefully styled and facial hair neatly trimmed. His coat rested on the back of his chair, a Sounders beanie stuffed in the pocket.

Cassandra pulled in a breath and stepped up to the table.

"I'm kind of surprised you actually came," Jacob remarked.

She draped her scarf over the back of the chair. "Me too," she admitted. "But Spencer told me it was a good idea."

The dig found its mark, and Jacob pressed his lips together in a forced smile.

It wasn't a lie. When Cassandra received Jacob's text saying that he would like to get coffee before he return to Spokane for the holiday, Spencer *had* told her she should go; he'd said that they couldn't afford to lose any support within the town, and as he wasn't about to become a possessive boyfriend, he was perfectly happy to let her meet with Jacob as a sign of goodwill.

Back when Jacob moved to town a month ago, he'd offered his help. Granted, he didn't know then what sort of help she needed, nor what he could offer. He said he wanted to be of whatever use he could be to her . . . because he still loved her.

Somehow, Cassandra didn't believe him. She'd never thought Jacob *really* loved her. Oh, he loved the idea of her—the thought that he could marry his best friend's sister, becoming true family with Isaac. He loved the idea that his parents and Cassandra's parents were also best friends. He loved the idea of raising his kids alongside Isaac's kids.

But Cassandra didn't think he actually loved *her*.

Still, she knew Spencer was right. They were working to protect DeVerre, turning it back into a safe, happy town. Having Jacob—who was now one of the few teachers left—on their side could impact their success through the years. He would have a positive influence on future generations of DeVerre. Any and every ally they could find would be a boon. Especially as the Warden continually pushed their way in.

After getting a decaf Americano from the barista, Cassandra took her seat across from Jacob. "Well," she said, the cardboard cup warm in her hands. "How've you been?"

Jake stared past her out the window. Her detail sat out there in their black sedan, watching for any sign that she needed their intervention. She doubted she'd need it here, but they were ever vigilant.

At last, his blue eyes shifted to hers. "I've been well," he said awkwardly. "How about you? How are you doing with . . . ?" His gaze drifted to the window once again, and she knew what he was asking.

Few people in DeVerre knew about the Spectral. The Warden had kept that information tightly shored up. But there was no hiding the way Cassandra was followed around at all times. So, they'd put out a palatable lie: Because of her family's Druidic background and Cassandra's rejection of them, there was concern for her safety, believing that perhaps the Druids would retaliate. After all, Debbie had tried to kill her.

That's what they'd chosen to tell the town that fateful morning. The Druids wanted Cassandra dead because, with the Varon brothers' help, she'd uncovered them. It was the truth, albeit selective.

With a wry smile, Cassandra lifted her coffee for a sip. "I'm just fine," she said.

"I'm glad to hear it," Jacob replied.

There was a prolonged, awkward silence.

Jacob picked at the sleeve of his cup. "Since you accepted my invitation," he said at last, "I'm guessing you're ready to accept my help."

"I suppose that depends on what kind of help you can offer," Cassandra said, though she had little interest in accepting anything he had to offer her.

"Well, I wasn't sure before," he admitted. "I know I can't protect you like—like your friends can. But I do have some other ideas now."

She nodded for him to go ahead.

"Well, obviously, the town has gone through a lot. And this, uh— Sheraton Corporation, right? That's the organization's name?"

Cassandra ducked her chin at the name of the Warden's shell corporation. "Right."

"Well, they're helping restructure the town. But I've noticed that some of the original townspeople aren't exactly thrilled with their influence."

Cassandra had noticed that as well. Tom and Sam had kept them apprised of several dissenting DeVerreans who questioned if things were truly better now. After all, no family had been left untouched by the deaths at the Veil. The Druids' roots had dug deep within DeVerre.

But all in all, the townspeople had taken the truth with somber but gracious fervor. There were bound to be bumps along the way—the very reason for Jeremiah Rhader's presence—but it seemed that things would turn out for the best. So long as they could squash any dissension in the ranks.

"However," Jacob said, almost excitedly, "I'm in a unique position. As I'm new to town and *not* a member of Sheraton Corp or your team at Occasus, people are more apt to talk to me. They're trying to get me on their side."

Cassandra frowned. "There are different sides?"

"Seems that way. I've had five separate groups reach out to me."

"Why you?"

He shrugged. "I guess I'm a swing vote or something. I don't think I'm the only one."

Cassandra chewed on the inside of her cheek. "What groups?"

"Sheraton, actually. They wanted me to join their teachers' union or something. But then, Gabe's militia too. Family members of deceased Druids who want their status back in the town. Family of those hurt by the Druids. And then . . ." He gave her a meaningful look then. "A group who call themselves the Scion."

Her brow wrinkled at the name. "And what do they want?" she asked.

Jacob took a deep breath. "They're the children of the Druids, apparently," he said. "And . . . they want to take back control of DeVerre."

Cassandra dropped her face into her hands. Some of the kids they'd taken cookies to that morning were staging a coup. Connor had warned them that some of the teens considered themselves to be Druids, but she remembered little Lindsey Frossard glaring at them and making some strange movement with her fingers as though marking them with a curse. Was it possible that those children really believed they could take back the town?

Cassandra looked back up at Jacob. "And why do they want *your* help?"

"I'm their teacher," he said. "I'm not a member of Sheraton, and I'm not a member of your group. But—and chalk this up to small-town gossip, okay?—there has been talk that you and I were involved. And they think that I can convince you to support them."

"Why would *I*—?"

"You're a Sauveterre," he said simply. "Apparently, that means something to them because they keep calling you 'the chosen one.'"

A tremor worked through Cassandra's hands. She gripped her coffee more firmly to still the movement.

"It also helps that they believe that that one guy living with you—Connor? They think he's playing you all. They believe he's planning to take back leadership and that getting in with *you* is his whole goal."

Shaking her head, Cassandra tried to fathom it all. These kids thought that Connor had defected as a backup plan to ensure the Druids won her over. They believed that she was "chosen," which meant they knew she was a Vessel, and since Lily was dead, the Spectral had no other host to attach to. Perhaps this was all information they'd presumed from things their parents told them in the past, but it didn't sit well with her.

Cassandra scanned Jacob across from her. He waited patiently, his steady blue gaze impressing her with the meaning behind his words. These kids had requested his help because they knew he had a past relationship with Cassandra. They thought he could get in with her. And he was offering to help. . . .

With a nod, Cassandra realized his intent. "So, meeting with me is an opportunity to convince them that you have a chance to do what they want," she said. "You're offering to play double agent?"

"I'm offering," Jacob sat forward, his eyes locked with hers, "to do whatever will keep you safe."

The other sentiment was plain in his gaze. He was willing to do this—to play informant—because he still had feelings for her. Because he hoped that it would prove himself to her. And more, that it would win her back.

Cassandra turned away with a sigh. This was ridiculous. There was a group of potentially dangerous teenagers raised by cultists looking to overthrow a town. And Jacob was offering to be their double agent to prove his love to her. It was foolish.

And yet, Cassandra couldn't help but see the merit in it. If these Druidic children were dedicated to their parents' cause, it would behoove them all to keep an eye on their actions.

Cassandra pressed her lips together, begrudgingly recognizing the importance of the offer. "I'll talk with Spencer and Peter," she said. "They'll have a better idea of how to handle this than I."

"You can make decisions for yourself, Cass."

She gave an annoyed frown at the abrasive inflection of his tone. "Yeah, I can. But I'm notoriously bad with people, Jake. Peter and Spencer are known for engendering trust and loyalty. They'll know how to handle a situation like this."

Jacob's shuttered expression showed his agitation—he didn't like that she was letting the brothers dictate this decision. Maybe for honorable reasons; perhaps he thought she deserved to make her own choices. Or maybe it was simply because he worried that Spencer would deny the offer on the principle that he didn't want Jacob and Cassandra spending more time together.

If she were being honest, Cassandra *hoped* Spencer would reject the idea because that's precisely how this would have to play out. If Jacob were going to be their double agent, he and Cassandra would have to spend time together. Alone. That would be the only way to convince the kids that he was actually valuable, that he could fulfill the role they'd set out for him. That he could win Cassandra back.

Annoyed by the idea, Cassandra pushed back from the table. The night had come in full now. "I've got to get back," she said.

"Yeah." Jacob stood too. "I ought to head out. The drive to Spokane isn't fun in the dark, but . . . I'm glad we did this. And thank you for considering my offer."

With a single nod, Cassandra draped her scarf back around her neck. "Merry Christmas."

Jacob took a step forward as though to hug her, then stopped himself when she bristled. He gave a sad smile. "Merry Christmas, Cass."

Cassandra didn't bother waiting. She turned, half-full coffee cup in hand, and pushed out the door.

~

"That's weird," Peter said, dropping the tubes of wrapping paper on the coffee table. "Does he really think it'll work?"

Cassandra divided the wrapping supplies into three piles for each of them: tape, scissors, tags, and string. Connor had begged out of their movie-and-gift-wrapping night to do more studying in his room. And Cassandra had taken the time without his presence to inform Peter and Spencer of Jacob's plan. It wasn't that she didn't trust Connor; she just wanted the brothers' thoughts without hearing the biased opinion of an ex-Druid yet.

"Which part?" Cassandra said sourly. "The being a double agent part? Or the convincing me to fall in love with him part?"

Peter scoffed in mocking humor while Spencer shook his head, focused on setting up the movie.

"Either," Peter said.

Cassandra grabbed her set of supplies and a tub of wrapping paper. "Probably. I don't know why he'd offer otherwise."

Spencer rose from his task, and the DVD's home screen came to life with Die Hard's ominous theme and clips from the film. Nex trailed at his side. "He could just be a nice guy," he said magnanimously.

"So you don't have any problem with me regularly hanging out with my ex, who has point-blank told me that he wants me back?" Cassandra asked, brow raised.

With a sly grin, he replied, "I told you I'm not the jealous type. If you think it's a good idea, I do too. But if you don't, or if you aren't comfortable with it, we can find another way to keep an eye on those kids."

She sighed at his goodness. "It isn't that I think it's a bad idea. I'm not about to catch feelings for him after all this time. But I don't *want* to spend time with him like that."

"Then we'll find another way."

"What other way?"

Spencer shrugged, confirming what Cassandra already knew. This was their best option. They could talk to the Warden and attempt to find another way, but because of her past with Jacob, they could easily win the Scions' confidence. There would be no assurances that the teens would accept any other individual into their ranks, aside from maybe Connor. But she didn't think he'd want the role, even if he didn't have to return to Spokane for medical school.

Peter's gaze bounced between Spencer and Cassandra before he spoke up. "Not trying to butt in on your relationship or anything, but if you want my opinion . . . I think this is our best bet. And it doesn't have to be a big deal either."

The couple looked at him, waiting for him to explain.

"Think about it—" Peter held out his hands. "You don't have to see him that often, Cass. It could be, like, once every couple of weeks or something. Maybe even less. I doubt he'll have information that often, anyway. And these kids know you're dating Spencer. It isn't like they'll expect you to throw him over after one coffee date. But the very fact that you're willing to meet may be enough to convince them that Jacob's chances are viable. Which is really all we need to make his mission a success."

Cassandra grimaced, thinking of Jacob as some secret agent on a mission. It seemed ridiculous.

In the background, the DVD's main screen looped around for the dozenth time, playing that haunting jingle bell theme, and Cassandra decided she was done with the conversation. They were supposed to be celebrating, reliving the Collins family's yearly traditions. She wasn't going to worry about what Jacob wanted from her or what these Druidic teens had planned. For now, she would wrap gifts and enjoy the company of her two favorite people.

"We can make this choice another time. It's Christmas, and we've got gifts to wrap. Now," Cassandra gestured with the tube of wrapping paper, "where should we set up? And just know, I will not abide by peeking. I catch you, and your gift gets returned."

Passing a grin to each other, Peter and Spencer gathered their own supplies. Spencer set himself up behind the couch nearest the office while Peter went around the other nearest the front door, leaving Cassandra to work at the coffee table. Anguis and Nex both settled in front of the fireplace, near her. Spencer hit play on the movie, and the opening credits rolled.

"You don't like flyin', do you?" Peter quoted along with the first line.

Spencer immediately threw a wad of extra box stuffing over the couches, just grazing Peter's head. "Shut up," Spencer said. "If they wanted to cast you, they would've done it."

"I wasn't born yet," Peter returned. "They didn't have a chance."

Cassandra rolled her eyes but smiled, enjoying Peter's regular quoting during the film, happy to be part of their tradition. She'd always liked wrapping gifts, but this year was special. She'd never had a boyfriend to give a gift. (Her relationship with Jacob ended before his birthday or Christmas came around.) And aside from Diane, she'd never known anyone well enough to feel proud of the gifts she'd chosen to give. Her family just shopped off lists. But with Peter and Spencer, she'd made her selections based on what she *knew* they'd like. Gifts that had special meaning.

Tying off the string on Spencer's first gift, Cassandra felt her heart warm. Peter began quoting again, but this time, Spencer joined him for a couple of lines as though in compulsion. Unable to see them, she chuckled at their antics.

By the light of the fire and the television, she was more content than she'd been in years. No matter how hard this last year had been, no matter how uncertain her future as the Vessel was, her relationship with Spencer and her life here in DeVerre had truly made her happy. And even if she had to go to Spokane and face her family tomorrow, she knew this Christmas would be the best she'd had yet.

Spencer

The morning of December 23—or Christmas Eve Eve as Peter liked to call it—they packed their bags and prepared to head to Spokane. As Spencer had suggested, they'd kept up their workout routine, making sure to stop in at the gym before wrapping up the last details before their trip. It was a roughly two-hour drive to the city, so they left just after lunch to ensure they didn't arrive too early.

With a final goodbye to Connor and the dogs, they piled into the Jeep and headed out under the overcast winter sky. The light was gray, and the roads were mostly empty, as they always were until they got closer to civilization. Spencer drove, but Cassandra insisted on sitting in the back. "If I can't drive on longer trips like this, I like room to stretch out," she said.

Peter made sure to trade out the CDs from Sting's Greatest Hits for his Christmas album. Though neither of them would consider Sting to be their favorite artist, he had been their dad's. As the Jeep had been David Collins's prized possession, they kept his music playing in his honor.

Spencer glanced in the rearview mirror, catching a glimpse of Cassandra. She lounged with her feet propped on the center console, phone in hand, as she read the *Wenzel & Frankly* Christmas Special. This was the first time she'd left DeVerre since the release of the Spectral, and they'd had to work extremely hard to keep her detail from coming with her.

When they'd told Rhader of their plans to leave town, he'd demanded they take at least one extra man to ensure her safety. Knowing how awkward the visit would be on its own, Spencer wouldn't stand for a bodyguard to make the situation even worse.

"Look," he'd told Rhader. "If anyone is going to keep Cassandra safe, it's me."

"You're going away from the Veil," the man had objected. "It's harder to wield the farther away you get."

"But we're Varons," Spencer said. "Peter and I won't let anything happen to her."

Rhader's dark eyes pierced his. "You may be Varons, but you're still new Wielders. You aren't experienced enough to defend where the Veil doesn't touch."

"But we are strong enough," Spencer countered. "Pete's the true Varon, right? That gives him extra power. And I'm her boyfriend. Trust me, that means I'd die before letting her get hurt."

That caused Rhader to pause, even as his jaw remained set.

Spencer pressed his advantage. "This trip wasn't planned," he said. "We decided to go this week, and we haven't told anyone but you, Connor, the Lamberts, and the Bernards. Which of us do you think will tell the Druids? And even if someone else figured it out, how quickly do you think they can prepare a strong enough attack away from the Veil?"

"It's dangerous," Rhader maintained.

"It's Christmas," Spencer returned. "And I won't let them take her."

Rhader must have seen the determination in Spencer's gaze because the man's countenance eased, and he dipped his chin. Then he'd given

Spencer pointers on connecting to the spirit world out of the radius of a Veil. It wasn't impossible, but it was more difficult. And he wanted to be sure that should they need to wield, they could. And while he'd agreed not to send a bodyguard *with* them, he insisted that he'd send two men to Spokane to stay at a nearby hotel should they need backup.

Spencer turned onto the main highway toward the city. He'd meant it when he told Rhader he wasn't afraid of an attack from the Druids. Not only did it seem unlikely, but he was too preoccupied with his other concern.

He was going to meet his girlfriend's parents.

Spencer had never had a serious enough relationship for that step. He wasn't really sure his past experiences could be considered relationships at all. He'd taken a few girls out on dates, he'd even worked up the gumption to kiss a couple of them, but none of them had stuck for longer than a month. Most of the time, it was less.

He'd already beaten that record with Cassandra. What was more, he knew, however fast it seemed, that he wanted to spend the rest of his life with her. Spectral or no Spectral, he'd promised that. He didn't think she realized that he'd meant it so committedly, but he did. No matter what came, if Cassandra would have him, Spencer would spend the rest of his life at her side, caring for her, protecting her, loving her.

The thought bolstered Spencer as they got closer and closer to Spokane. The gray sky grew darker as the early evening crept in, a gentle snow beginning to cascade from the clouds. Driving through the city, his body began to tighten with anxiety. His muscles tremored slightly when he thought about meeting Allen and Julianne Clement. He'd heard so little about them beyond their unsupportive and manipulative ways from Cassandra and insignificant details from Peter's short experience over a month ago.

Spencer wasn't sure what to believe. He knew that Cassandra wasn't intentionally painting them as villains, but he had a hard time believing they were that bad. He hoped he wasn't wrong.

Pulling into the driveway, Spencer scanned the pretty house in the fading light of day. It glowed like a beacon. Lights lined its roof and the wrought iron rails on the porch steps. More lights covered the bushes out front, and a white-painted wooden nativity set was displayed with a spotlight all its own. Even the wreath on the door was lit up with tiny lights.

Peter and Spencer grabbed the luggage from the trunk while Cassandra stood anxiously to the side. Spencer would have taken her hand to comfort her, but she moved for the door before he could. He slung his backpack over his shoulder and hefted her duffel with the other hand, hurrying to follow behind her.

As though they'd been watching for them, Allen and Julianne met them at the door. They looked surprisingly normal to Spencer after every negative thing he'd heard. Allen had dark hair, graying at the temples, and a well-kept beard, more white than brown at this point. He looked quite a bit like his daughter with their broad foreheads, slim noses, high cheekbones, and square jawlines. But Cassandra shared her mother's sharply arched brows and down-turned lips that seemed to betray their emotions without their own knowledge.

What was decidedly different between mother and daughter was their eye color. Cassandra had those verigated hazel eyes, while Julianne's were crystal clear blue. Beyond that, Julianne's accident months back had damaged her left eye, leaving it blinded. Three slowly healing scars lingered on her temple and cheek, reminding them all of the price the Druids had exacted for Cassandra's defiance.

The Clements readily welcomed them into the heated house. It smelled of hearty beef and warm spices, like a Christmas roast. Spencer's cheeks tingled from the cold exterior, an awkward air filling the entry as forced smiles and kind greetings were exchanged. Spencer squirmed slightly under Julianne's intent stare. From the moment he'd stepped in, her gaze had locked on him as though sizing him up.

After hugging Cassandra, Allen turned to the brothers. "Nice to see you again, Peter," Allen said.

"Same," Peter replied, shaking his hand.

"And you must be Spencer," Julianne said, her voice threaded with tension.

"Yes, ma'am," Spencer said, remembering his southern roots in Virginia. Though none of his family carried notable accents, most of them either from the military or, like their mom, from other states themselves, he'd still learned the cultural politeness. "It's a pleasure to meet you both."

Allen shook his hand next, his smile not quite meeting his eyes. "And you," he said. "I'd say we've heard so much about you, but . . ."

He'd made the remark good-naturedly, but Cassandra pressed her lips together in agitation.

Spencer decided he should save the moment. "There's not much to hear," he said lightly. "I'm pretty boring, to be honest."

"I doubt that," Julianne said, her appraising stare still on him. "Cassie never was much for the mundane."

Spencer tossed Cassandra a smirk. "I can believe that."

Cassandra sent him a knowing smile, a soft glimmer in her eyes.

A stilted silence passed before Allen spoke again. "Is this all your things?" he asked, gesturing to the backpacks and duffels Peter and Spencer carried. "Or is there more I can help bring in?"

"Nah, this is it," Peter said. "We pack light."

"It is just a night," Cassandra added.

"Of course," Julianne said, stepping back. "Allen, why don't you show the boys to their rooms and drop off Cassie's things while you're up there? Dinner is just about ready, so, Cassandra, dear, would you help me set the table?"

Cassandra hesitated but nodded. Spencer passed her an encouraging look before they parted ways. He wanted her to know she wasn't alone, even if they would be separate for these few minutes. She didn't have to fear the pressures her parents had placed on her in the past. He'd be right there to remind her where she truly belonged.

While Cassandra followed her mom into the kitchen, Allen led the brothers to the stairs. The Clement house was cozy, filled with holiday decorations. It was clear that they valued Christmas. Every nook and cranny held some display. It even seemed they had changed the pictures around their house to match the season, as wintry landscapes and understated Christmas paintings adorned the walls. There was one gallery of photos that looked permanent, however.

On the wall leading to the second floor were picture after picture of the Clement family. Spencer paused, catching sight of a little version of Cassandra in an emerald-green velvet dress with a huge white collar that had a black satin ribbon woven through the lace. A matching velvet headband held back her dark hair, a massive smile on her face that showed off her missing front teeth.

Spencer forced himself to continue up the stairs even as he gazed at the gallery. There were dozens more photos like that, spanning several years, displaying Cassandra's childhood as well as her brother, Isaac. He caught sight of Jacob in a handful of photos too. Then he saw one with Jacob and Cassandra together, his arm around her affectionately as they sat on a couch, and Spencer decided he'd lost interest.

Allen guided Spencer and Peter to the guest room at the far end of the second floor, dropping Cassandra's bag off in her room down the hall. He told them their room used to be Isaac's until he moved out during college. They'd turned it into a study for Allen with a spare bed for guests, which was why it felt somewhat cluttered with the desk, bookshelves, and other bedroom furnishings.

"The bathroom is next to Cassandra," Allen explained, standing at the threshold. "Feel free to take a few minutes to unpack or get comfortable. Whatever you prefer. It'll be a few minutes before dinner is ready."

"Thanks," Spencer said, taking the lead he would usually abdicate to Peter. As this was *his* girlfriend's family, he wanted to be the one to stand out.

He set his backpack on the foot of the bed, then gestured to the bookshelves. "I see you're a Robert Ludlum fan."

Allen glanced at the shelves, a grin coming to his lips. "Ah, yes," he said with a chuckle. "I enjoy his work. Though I'm partial to Lee Child."

Trying to remember which books Child wrote, Spencer nodded. He cast a sideways glance at the shelves but didn't recognize any of the titles offhand. "That's cool," he said, glad to know Cassandra's dad was a reader. At least, that boded well for his respect for Spencer's chosen career.

"If you want to talk books," Allen said, "you should really speak with Isaac. He's the reader of our family, always going on about some fantasy series or another."

Spencer and Peter exchanged an excited look. Though Isaac and his wife wouldn't join them until the morning, the knowledge that they'd have a bibliophile to talk shop with was a good sign.

Returning downstairs, they found Cassandra in the dining room, setting utensils by each of the plates.

In short order, Allen and Julianne brought in the meal. Spencer had guessed correctly; the dinner was a roast, cooked with well-seasoned carrots and onions. While Allen set the enamel-coated cast-iron pot on the candy-cane-striped trivet in the center of the table, Julianne carried in a gravy boat and a ceramic bowl heaped with mashed potatoes. Allen served their beverages, and she settled another bowl of steamed green beans and a basket of rolls on the snowflake embroidered tablecloth.

Once they were all seated at the dinner table, Allen said a prayer of thanks for the meal and their company, and the not-so-subtle investigation began.

"So, Spencer," Allen said as he served the roast, "what is it you do for work?"

"I'm a writer," Spencer said, amazed that for the first time in his life, it was true. "Actually, Pete and I write together."

"What is it that you write?" Julianne asked, and he couldn't tell whether she was truly intrigued or just being polite.

Spencer settled his napkin onto his lap the way he'd seen the Clements do. "Paranormal mysteries. At the moment, we have a decent following on our serial blog, but we're looking to switch to publishing novels starting this next year."

"Is that lucrative?" Allen asked.

"Dad," Cassandra lamented.

"I'm not asking about his prospects, Cass. I'm genuinely curious. We have a few author clients at the firm, but I don't work on their accounts much. I do know they're both with major publishing houses." Allen turned to Spencer and Peter. "Do you have a publisher?"

"Nah, we're doing it on our own," Peter said. "We want creative control, and though it's more work in the short term, if you do it right, you can actually make way more money."

"How interesting." Allen ladled some potatoes and carrots onto Cassandra's plate before handing it back to her. "Well, if you already have a following, I'd imagine that will be beneficial when it comes time to release your first book."

"That's the hope," Peter confirmed.

"Pardon my ignorance," Julianne said. "But what is a paranormal mystery?"

Spencer and Peter shared a smile. They'd gotten that question more times than they could count. After explaining the rough plot line of *Wenzel & Frankly*, Spencer added, "It's like *Sherlock Holmes* but with werewolves, vampires, and monsters." Then he realized how unprofessional that sounded compared to Allen's job working at an accounting firm.

Julianne's baffled expression confirmed that she thought so too. "Oh," she said lightly. "Well, that sounds . . . charming."

"It is," Cassandra said immediately. "Diane and I read the serial together for years before I met Spencer and Peter. It's excellent."

"That's great," Allen said, then, to Spencer's relief, moved the conversation forward. "And why did you two decide to move to DeVerre?"

"Well . . ." Spencer and Peter shared a look. "Diane left us her estate, so we saw it as our opportunity to pursue our careers."

"Where are you from originally?"

"Norfolk, Virginia."

"Isn't that near the ocean?" Julianne asked.

"Yeah, there were a bunch of beaches just a few miles from where we lived."

"That sounds lovely."

"They are. Though to be honest, Pete and I didn't go very often."

"You can tell by how pale we are," Peter added.

Julianne actually let out a genuine chuckle, her scars puckering slightly. "Oh, you fit in just fine with us 'Toners."

Unsure what the term meant, Spencer and Peter both smiled and nodded anyway.

"Do you have family in Norfolk?" Julianne asked.

"Yeah, most of our family is there," Spencer confirmed. "Our mom and stepdad, plus all our aunts, uncles, and cousins."

"Who are adoptive," Peter added, "as we recently learned."

Allen and Julianne wore surprised expressions. "You were adopted?" Julianne asked.

"Oh, no." Peter laughed. "Sorry. Our grandfather and Diane, our great-aunt—*they* were adopted. So, our dad—he was born a Collins, but our real family, the Varons, actually came from DeVerre."

Julianne blanched. "Varons?"

Spencer suddenly remembered that Julianne had grown up in DeVerre as the daughter of a Druid. He glanced at Cassandra, then answered, "Yes. Our great-grandfather was Michael Varon."

"That's . . ." Julianne looked between Spencer and her daughter, then to her husband, shifting uncomfortably in her seat. She brushed absentmindedly at the scars on the side of her face.

Allen set his fork down, reaching over to take her hand. "Julie?"

Julianne attempted a small smile. "It's fine," she said. "My, uh—my father said that the Varon line had ended, that's all. And it's surprising to, um . . . It's surprising."

Spencer gave her a compassionate smile while Peter took a sip of his water.

Cassandra, however, didn't take pity on her mother. "The Sauveterres helped kill Michael and his wife, Seraphine," she said. "So what I think Mom means is that her father bragged about how they murdered Peter and Spencer's family."

"My father was only a year old when Michael died," Julianne immediately defended. "He had nothing to do with it."

"But he would have," Cassandra returned. "If he had been old enough."

Spencer immediately set his hand on Cassandra's thigh under the table. She met his gaze, and he gave his unspoken warning.

Then, he turned to Julianne. "That's in the past," he said. "And Pete and I are ready to leave it there."

Julianne's sharp stare twitched, her expression unsure.

Spencer gave her a kind smile before turning to Allen. "Cass said that Isaac works with you at the accounting firm," he prompted, helping move the conversation forward.

Allen took the opportunity. "Yes, he's following in my footsteps, that's for sure. Went straight into college for an accounting degree and came out ready to take on the world." He gave a half-hearted chuckle. "The guys at the firm will tell you that Ike's a chip off the old block, but he's more like his mother. He got her determination and willpower."

A gentle smile pulled at Julianne's lips at the likely routine compliment.

Spencer smiled, too, remembering how their dad used to say similar things about their own mother. However, David Collins was more likely to say that Mallory was devoted and endearingly quirky.

The rest of the meal, they discussed Spencer and Peter's family, their time in college, and other tidbits about their lives. They asked about how they were settling into DeVerre and how nice it was of them to give Cassandra a place to stay after the situation with Debbie, which brought another bout of awkward silence.

Spencer and Peter asked about Allen and Julianne's lives in Spokane. They learned that Julianne worked part-time at their church and taught piano lessons to a few children. At which point, they also learned that Cassandra could play and had minored in music at college.

"I haven't played in years," Cassandra said when they looked at her in awed shock.

"Why not?" Spencer asked.

She shrugged. "There wasn't really an opportunity."

Peter used his fork to point at Spencer. "We could fit a piano in the living room turret, right?" he asked.

"Probably," Spencer said.

"No—" Cassandra shook her head. "You guys aren't buying a piano just for me."

"Sure, we are," Peter said happily.

"Besides," Spencer added with a dry grin, "it isn't just for you. It's for us to listen to you."

She rolled her eyes, but he could see the idea pleased her.

Allen and Julianne watched the exchange with something like uncertainty. Spencer wasn't sure what would make them hesitant about the brothers buying Cassandra a piano, but then he realized they probably didn't understand the kind of dedication Peter and he felt for their daughter.

It was another reason Spencer hung back while Peter and Cassandra helped Juliane clear the table. He carefully stepped closer to Allen and whispered, "Do you have a minute?"

In the middle of gathering the unused utensils, Allen paused. He glanced toward the kitchen, then faced Spencer. "For a private conversation?" he surmised.

"Yes, sir," Spencer said, his anxiety causing his fingers to fidget at his side.

Allen straightened. "Sure. Why don't we go up to your room?"

Spencer nodded, letting Allen lead the way. He knew this conversation would be unexpected and fast, but he didn't know when would be better to have it. After all, Isaac and his family were coming in the morning. There wouldn't be enough time. If he wanted to be upfront with Cassandra's dad, now was the time.

Once in the guest room, Allen took a seat in his desk chair while Spencer stood by the bookshelf. He'd partially shut the door, leaving it ajar. Allen waited expectantly, his dark brows drawn low.

Resting one elbow on the shelf beside him, Spencer clasped his hands before him. "I'll keep this short," he said, knowing he had two equally important topics to discuss. "When Cassandra told me about your invitation, I convinced her to come."

Allen raised his chin knowingly. "I wondered," he admitted.

"You did?"

He nodded. "Over the last month, I've contacted Cassandra a handful of times. She's ignored each one."

Spencer took a deep breath. He didn't know whether to be proud of her for setting boundaries or bothered by how set against her family she was. "She's hurt."

"Understandably," Allen said matter-of-factly with no edge of malice or self-pity.

"I'm glad you see it that way." Spencer massaged his palm. "I'll admit, I wanted to be sure you did. But that's not the primary reason I wanted to talk with you. Though I'd be happy to discuss it more at length another time, if you'd like."

Allen's dark gaze narrowed thoughtfully. "What did you want to talk about?"

Spencer shifted on his feet, forcing his hands to his sides. He held the man's stare determinedly. "I wanted to tell you that I care about your daughter," he said. "Very much. And while we haven't been together long, I take our relationship quite seriously."

Allen listened, seeming to know Spencer wasn't done.

He swallowed down the last of his anxiety and said what he needed to say, "And I want you to know I intend to marry her."

Allen's eyes went wide at that, no doubt shocked at the quick determination. They'd only been dating for a month, after all. That was fast by anyone's standards. "Are you asking for my permission?" he asked.

Spencer blanched. "Oh, no—no, I'm not planning to propose yet, I just—I wanted you to know my intentions." He forced his heart rate to return to a normal rhythm as he continued, "Because one day, I *will* come to ask you for your blessing, and on that day, I don't want there to be any doubts in your mind about whether or not I mean it."

"I see." Allen shifted in his seat.

Spencer couldn't tell the man's feelings about his confession. He was contained and calm despite his tense posture. As far as Spencer could tell, Allen could either be angered, disappointed, bemused, or simply unsure how to proceed.

After several moments, Allen sighed gently. "Well, as a father, I can tell you that makes me glad to hear," he said, then shook his head. "I know that Julie and I haven't always been the most . . . supportive parents. But everything we've done has been out of love for our daughter. As misguided as our actions may have been."

"I understand that," Spencer said honestly. "And I believe that despite all the hurt Cassandra feels, the love of a parent is irreplaceable."

Allen tipped his head to the side, clearly surprised.

"I come from a really amazing family," Spencer continued. "My dad and mom were pretty much the greatest parents the world has ever seen. And when my dad died, it . . . It sort of destroyed Pete and me."

Allen's expression pinched sympathetically.

"I know what it's like to lose your family," Spencer said. "Cassandra doesn't. And though she's ready to give up on you all, I won't let her. Because no matter how screwed up everything you've done is . . . family is the most important thing in this world. And I won't let her lose that."

Allen began to smile appreciatively, but Spencer wasn't done. "That said," he let his tone grow firm, "I won't let you hurt her any more than you already have. So, if this becomes another situation where you try to dictate how she lives her life or where you shame her for what she does or doesn't do . . . I *will* support her decision to cut you off entirely."

A heavy acceptance drew Allen's shoulders down. "I understand," he promised.

"Great." Spencer took a step back toward the door. "Thanks for talking with me."

Allen held up a forestalling hand. "You've shared your intentions," he said, an adamance in his expression. "Now may I share mine?"

Spencer came to a stop, ready to hear Allen's words.

"Julie and I love our daughter. Perhaps incorrectly, but we love her all the same. And we want to correct the errors of our past relationship with her."

Allen sat forward in his seat to impress his following words on Spencer. "This is our attempt at making restitution. *Our* intention is to prove that to her." He held his stare determinedly. "And I'd very much appreciate your help in that."

"I already told you," Spencer said. "I won't let her lose her family. So long as you behave as a family should, I'll have no problem supporting you in that."

Allen nodded slowly. "Then you have our gratitude," he said, paused, and then added, "And should everything continue as it seems—should you be as good for Cassandra as you seem . . . I will have no problem giving you my blessing whenever you make that choice."

A tingle raced down Spencer's spine at the thought. Had it been this simple? Had mere honesty been enough to convince Allen Clement of Spencer's worthiness of his daughter? But then, he realized that wasn't all his honesty had given.

Allen wasn't lying when he said that he wanted the best for his daughter. He'd wrongly tried to control Cassandra in the past, but it had never been for personal gain. It had been out of misguided love and an attempt at protection. And now, Spencer's honesty had given Allen the one thing he hoped for: the knowledge that Cassandra was cared for, safe, and happy.

Spencer smiled. "I'll look forward to it."

CHAPTER TWELVE

Connor

Connor sat in his SUV, the blasting heat searing his cheeks as he stared at the front of the Bernard house. Winter plants hung from the porch, a little bench off to the side. He and Anna had spent countless hours out there during their youth. Thin strands of Christmas lights edged the porch's eaves and rail as though to highlight the house that used to bring him so much joy.

Tapping his fingers on the steering wheel, Connor debated returning to Occasus. He shouldn't be here. Movie nights were a Friday night Lambert family tradition, even beyond Christmastime. No matter if some of them were busy with work or other responsibilities, the rest gathered together to eat popcorn, drink tea, and snuggle on the couch to watch their favorite classics.

Connor had once been a part of that tradition. But it had been years.

As Christmas Eve was on a Friday this year, they'd moved the tradition to the twenty-third. Connor hadn't expected to be invited. But when he'd gone over to Aaron's that morning to hang out and play video games, he'd mentioned it to Connor.

"You comin' tonight?" he asked.

It took Connor a minute to realize what he was asking. "Oh, uh, I didn't realize I was invited."

"Of course you are. You've been invited since first grade."

Connor was thankful for the game to stare at to hide his instinctual flinch. "That was before medical school."

"You were still invited whenever you were in town. You just didn't show 'cause you were an idiot."

He forced himself not to grit his teeth. "I didn't come because I didn't want to put Anna in any more danger than she already was."

"I still can't believe your dad was such an ass," Aaron muttered. Then he paused the game and turned to Connor. "Dude, you're invited. You'll always be invited. No matter how stupid you get."

Connor tried to smile but knew it fell frighteningly short. "Thanks," he said genuinely. "But I don't think I should come."

Aaron began to protest, so Connor cut him off. "The other night was bad enough. I'm not going to ruin your family's Christmas."

Aaron begrudgingly let it go, and Connor thought it was the end of it.

Then he'd gotten a phone call from Ava that afternoon.

"What do you mean you're not coming?" she said instead of a greeting.

Connor sighed. "I think it'd be best—"

"You're coming. That's that."

"Ava, I appreciate—"

"Don't be a child, Connor. You've been invited to join our family for Christmas movie night. If you don't show up, it's because *you're* being weird, not us."

"I'm trying to be respectful," he defended.

"You're trying to protect yourself," she shot back. "Now, get your act together, or I'll have to drive to Occasus and drag your butt out into the cold myself. Got it?"

Knowing these were no idle threats, Connor forced himself to agree.

Now, he sat parked on the curb of Hope Court, staring at the daunting house, unable to get himself to move. He'd grown up in that house as much as his family's. It felt more like home than most places. And he missed it.

With a heavy sigh, Connor told himself to man up. These were the people he'd once considered family. They were the reason for everything he was doing. He owed it to them to bring Anna back and make this town what they'd always imagined it to be. And they *had* invited him to join, even if it was out of pity.

Connor forced himself up the porch steps and knocked on the front door. It didn't take even thirty seconds before it flung wide, revealing Haley on the other side. She tugged him in, calling out, "Connor's here."

A smattering of greetings came from the interior of the house. Aaron popped his head around the corner from the kitchen as Haley left Connor to hang his coat on the rack. Ava was already curled up on the couch with their gray cat, Eurydice, while Aimee sat on the antique loveseat, crocheting. Haley dropped down at her sister-in-law-to-be's side. That was part of the tradition. The men served the women on movie night.

At Aaron's beckoning wave, Connor made his way past the women, who chatted casually about the Lambert family in Canada, to the kitchen. When he stepped around the corner, he found Andrew dumping a bag of popcorn into a bowl while Owen pulled a second bag from the microwave. A kettle of tea steeped on the counter, the scent of cinnamon spice drifting from its steaming spout.

"Here," Aaron said, handing Connor a blue and white snowflake plate filled with peppermint bark. "You can take these in."

"He just got here, Aaron," his father scolded. "Let the man have a second."

Andrew turned his good-natured smile Connor's way then. "I heard the brothers and Cassandra left you alone up in that big old house of theirs."

Working hard to hold the man's gaze, Connor nodded. "Yes, sir. They, uh—they went to Spokane to visit her family."

"I don't think I could live in a house like that," Andrew said with a self-derisive chuckle. "Too spooky."

"It isn't as bad as you'd think," Owen said. "The guest room is actually pretty nice."

Connor had forgotten that Owen had stayed in the house—in the room Connor currently occupied—for the short stint of his and Ava's separation. He was further surprised that Owen would bring it up around Andrew. However, he supposed that Owen had had to come clean to his in-laws about his past lies. Connor himself had been shocked to learn that the Warden had orchestrated Owen's move to DeVerre. And for a moment, Connor didn't feel quite so bad, realizing that he wasn't the only one in the room who'd lied to this family for over a decade.

Choosing to make his time with the family less awkward, Connor asked, "What are we watching?"

"The 2004 *Christmas Carol*," Owen said.

"Aimee has a thing for Kelsey Grammer," Andrew added.

"I do not," Aimee called from the living room. "I just like seeing Frasier sing. It's hilarious."

"She does," Andrew mouthed.

Connor couldn't help smiling at the banter between the older couple. It was so much a part of his childhood that it felt right to witness it again. There was something comforting about watching Andrew and Aimee's sharp repartee, like an assurance that so long as they loved one another as they had when they were in their youth, there was hope for a marriage that was rich and wonderful.

Connor and Anna had never had that sort of banter. Their conversations were always filled with gentle teasing, easy compliments, and casual contemplations. In all his imagining, he knew their marriage wouldn't look quite like the Lamberts', but would be no less full of love and happiness.

The thought made his gut twist. Connor had imagined marrying Anna hundreds of times through the years. It'd been all that he'd dreamed of in high school. Connor had been a serious child who grew into a serious young man. It might have had something to do with being raised by Alexander and Giana Frossard, both of them demanding perfection from the moment of his birth. Or maybe it was his natural personality. But from the first moment he remembered seeing Anna Lambert at DeVerre chapel when he had only just turned five years old, he knew he'd marry her.

He could remember sitting on his knees, facing backward on the pew, peering at her over the wooden back. She sat between her brother and sister, the three of them playing some game on a piece of paper, giggling together as they waited for the service to start. It was Anna's smile that had captivated little Connor. It was so full and peaceful. Even in the three-pew distance between them, he could feel the smile all the way down to his soul.

When they'd started kindergarten together, Connor had to force himself not to stare at Anna all day, every day. He wanted to be her friend. He wanted to be at her side, soaking in the calm, peaceful quality she carried everywhere she went. But he'd been afraid.

For one thing, Anna was quiet. She didn't go out of her way to be noticed, and she was happy to follow the lead of others. Beyond that, there were only eight kids in the class; four boys—Connor, Hunter, Tyler, and Devon—and four girls—Anna, Regan, Krista, and Mary. And inevitably, the genders split into friend groups.

Connor was immediately elected as the leader of the boys. They all looked to him for everything, rarely leaving him alone to pursue a friendship with Anna. As Krista was the loudest and strongest-willed of the girls, she was the one to lead them. And Anna faded into the background as always, content to let her friends have the limelight while she sat to the side, coloring or listening.

It wasn't until he'd seen Krista bullying Anna that he'd had the opportunity to insert himself into her life. And from then on, he'd never left her side.

Connor was reasonably sure that's why neither of them wound up with many other friends from then on. The rest of the students grew closer while he and Anna became inseparable. They didn't need anyone else. They had each other.

Until they didn't.

And now, he'd ruined everything, and she was gone.

As Andrew finished dispersing the second bag of popcorn into the bowls, he said, "That about does it."

"Great." Aaron grabbed a bowl and a tray of peanut brittle. "Let's get this over with."

Connor and Owen shared an amused smirk. Aaron had always hated musicals.

Owen lifted the tea tray, weighted down with seven vintage Christmas teacups that matched the painted porcelain pot. It clinked gently as he followed Aaron.

Connor picked up the plate of peppermint bark, ready to follow, when Andrew caught his arm. "Hang on a second," he said, voice low.

A thread of panic wove through Connor's stomach. Was this it—the moment when Andrew quietly requested that he get out of his family's life? Had Connor's presence been too much? Should he leave now?

Connor swallowed the lump in his throat, trying not to let his worry show as he faced the man.

Andrew glanced toward the living room, releasing his hold on Connor. His dark blue gaze was intense as he spoke. "Before we start the movie, I wanted a word."

Connor nodded because he couldn't speak.

"Ava told me that she had to threaten you this afternoon," he said, brow rising. "She said you wouldn't come otherwise."

Connor nodded again.

"Mm." Andrew pressed his lips together, then sighed. "Well, then I think you should know: no matter what your parents did, no matter what struggles you've been through . . ." His expression softened as he smiled. "You're part of our family, Connor, and we will always love you."

The words washed over Connor like stepping into a heated house from so long in the frosted winter. It warmed him to his very core with its impossible goodness. It was everything he hadn't been brave enough to hope for.

"And once Anna's back with us," Andrew continued, "we look forward to calling you our true son."

Connor tried to swallow past the emotion building within him. The Christmas plate bit into his palm, and he realized he was holding it in a death grip. "I—" His voice caught as his brow furrowed. "I'm the reason she's dead."

Sorrow pinched Andrew's expression. "No. You're the reason she'll live again."

Andrew clapped his arm in a fatherly gesture. He smiled through the tears in his eyes. "We're counting on you," he said kindly. "Because we won't be complete without the two of you—together."

Unable to speak, Connor stared at Andrew with a gaping mouth. He felt locked, as though he'd been struck in the chest by an arc of the spirit world. But instead of leaving him hollow and in pain, he just felt trapped in time, unable to think or breathe because of the hope coursing through his veins.

Andrew seemed to understand Connor's silence. He let out a small chuckle, grabbed the remaining popcorn bowl, and gave him a gentle shove toward the living room.

Somehow, Connor's feet carried him forward. Andrew went to sit next to his wife on the loveseat while Aaron instructed Connor to take the open seat at his side. Owen handed him a cup of tea with honey already stirred in, just the way Connor liked it. Ava tossed Connor's favorite throw pillow at him, and Haley held out the blanket he and Anna always shared for movie nights in the past.

And for the first time in a long time, Connor felt like he'd come home.

Sitting there with the Lamberts and Bernards, Connor realized that no matter what family he'd been born into, this was where he truly belonged. Everything good in his life had been given to him by this family. They'd taught him to be honorable, kind, and considerate. Their love taught him to love. Where his parents might have turned him into a cold-blooded killer bent on bringing the spirit world upon the physical realm, Andrew and Aimee Lambert's family had helped him discover a whole other way of life.

Watching as Scrooge turned from a miser into a benefactor, Connor concluded that he wanted to be the sort of man the Lambert parents had raised him to be. One whom they'd be proud to call son. He desired to leave the world changed just as they'd changed his.

Long after the movie ended, Connor left the warm embrace of Owen and Ava's house. He darted through the frigid night to his car, hands tucked into his coat pockets, where his fingers brushed the red Mustang he'd forgotten was there. A startling thought whispered in the back of his mind. Without the Lamberts, he wouldn't have had the courage to be different from his parents. He didn't want to know who he'd be without their positive, loving influence. And it made him realize he was responsible for making that kind of difference in others' lives too.

His fingers tightened around the metal toy car.

It was his responsibility to make that difference in one particular life.

Getting in his Land Rover, Connor made the choice: He needed to raise Josiah. Not just mentor him as the Warden had asked. Just being around from time to time wasn't enough. He needed to be a father to the boy, to be what Andrew had been for him. It was his responsibility to teach Josiah how to be a good man, even if Connor wasn't always sure what that looked like.

The thought that Anna wouldn't want to adopt Josiah only lingered in Connor's thoughts for a second. If she were here, he was sure she would have made the suggestion herself.

Putting the SUV in gear, Connor smiled to himself. Tomorrow at the service, he would talk to Rhader, and somehow, he'd convince the man to let him adopt Josiah when he graduated. Whatever came, whether or not he saved Anna, this was his job as a Frossard and as a man. He could raise the boy meant to be a Druid, helping him become something far greater.

Spencer

If Spencer had thought the previous evening was awkward, it was only because he'd yet to experience the discomfort of the next morning.

The first hiccup came when they woke up. Sharing a bed with Peter had never been ideal, but they'd done it plenty of times in the past. Brothers put up with that sort of thing from time to time. They'd set their alarm to give them plenty of time to prepare before Cassandra's brother, Isaac, and his family arrived. But they'd forgotten to account for sharing the bathroom with Cassandra, making them run late.

When Cassandra finished up in the bathroom, Peter let Spencer shower first since it was *his* girlfriend's family they were meeting. Once he was all showered and dressed, Spencer opened the bathroom door to defog the mirror. He stared into the looking glass, weighing whether to risk shaving and delaying himself further.

Cassandra exited her old room, her hair and makeup freshly done. When she saw him, she drifted toward the bathroom to lean against the doorframe. "Morning," she said. Her long black sweater draped loosely around her torso, the left corner tucked into her black jeans. She wore black ankle socks to keep her feet warm on the wood floors.

Spencer repeated the greeting. "Why didn't you tell me to shave *before* we got here?" he asked in teasing agitation.

"Why would I?" she returned.

"Because I look like a bum," he said, keeping his voice low. "No wonder your dad thought I'm broke. If I saw myself on the street, I'd think about crossing to the other side."

Cassandra snorted in amusement. "It's nowhere near that bad," she said, stepping into the room. "Yeah, you've got some scruff, but I kind of like it."

"Glad you like hobo-chic."

"I'd call it rugged academic," she teased, brushing some of his overlong hair out of his eyes. "You look like you've been too busy writing your research paper and threw something so vapid as grooming out the window."

He chuckled softly, slipping an arm around her waist. "Yes, because all academics wear denim jackets."

She tugged on the sleeve of his navy sweater. "You're not wearing your jacket now."

"I was wearing it last night."

"And you looked like a woodsman then." She kissed his cheek, then pulled away. "A really hot woodsman."

He blew out a disbelieving snort. "No one has ever called *me* hot."

"Then they're blind." She arched a brow. "Or too nervous to be honest."

Spencer gave her a flat stare of disbelief.

She smirked and backed out of the room. "Leave the scruff," she said and winked. "I like it."

While she disappeared down the stairs, Spencer turned back to the mirror. He ran a hand through his slightly damp, outgrown hair. It now completely covered his ears, curling slightly. He needed to get a haircut before it started to hang over his collar.

Spencer sighed, forgoing the shave, and gathered his things to relinquish the bathroom to Peter. Then he followed Cassandra's path downstairs. The Clements were in the living room, husband and wife seated side by side on a loveseat facing away from the hall. They were quietly sipping their coffee, heads dipped as though reading.

Spencer found Cassandra in the kitchen. The smell of cinnamon and cream wafted through the air. Sausage links sizzled on the stovetop. Cassandra had her own mug of coffee—a monstrously splotchy blue, pink, and purple painted thing—as she sat at the island, reading her Bible.

She smiled as he walked over. "Feel free to get yourself a cup," she said, motioning to the coffee machine. "We'll make a second pot just before it's time to eat."

"Do I have to use a mug as ugly as yours?" Spencer teased.

She slugged his arm. "I painted this at a pottery shop, thank you very much."

"You chose pink?"

"I was ten." Cassandra rose from the counter and pulled a traditional Christmas mug from the cabinet. "Here," she said. "Use this, you critic."

Spencer continued smirking. "I just can't fathom that you ever liked bright colors."

Cassandra took her seat back at the island. "It was a short-lived phase."

Once Spencer had his coffee, he took the stool next to hers. He wished he had thought to bring his Bible along with him so he could read with her. But if he were honest, he wasn't even sure where his Bible was. Probably on the bookshelf in his room.

Sitting there in an awkward silence while Cassandra read, Spencer glanced over his shoulder into the living room. He could barely see Allen and Julianne, but he caught the movement of one of them turning a page. His brow raised as he realized they were reading their Bibles too.

Without thinking about it, Spencer began to ask, "Are your parents—?" before remembering that Cassandra was trying to read. "Sorry," he said as she looked up. "Never mind."

"It's okay," she said. "What were you going to ask?"

Feeling guilty, Spencer nodded toward the living room. "I was just surprised," he said. "I didn't realize your parents took their faith as seriously as you."

"Oh." Cassandra's gaze darted in her parents' direction. She sighed. "Yeah, they do. Honestly, it's always been kind of difficult for me, knowing that they love God and are still so unsupportive of me, *knowing* that I love Him too. But, yeah, they take their faith very seriously. I think that's why Mom chose to leave the Druids when she was a teen. She couldn't reconcile their beliefs with her own and so, she chose a separate path."

"Did she tell you that?"

"No. It's just a feeling I get. My entire life, Dad and Mom have done exactly that—" she gestured to the living room, "read their Bibles and prayed together on that loveseat before Dad goes to work. And I just can't imagine that's all made up. Even if they've made some very real mistakes."

Spencer ran his thumb along the handle of his coffee mug. "My parents did something similar," he said. "I remember one morning, I got up early and found them in the kitchen where Dad was reading aloud to Mom while she made breakfast. Mom always had trouble sitting down to read—she's like Peter. She struggles to sit still for long periods. Especially if what she's reading doesn't keep her attention. So, Dad would read the Bible to her so that she could actually take it in."

"That's really sweet," Cassandra said.

Spencer smiled. "Yeah. They were weirdly cute."

Gently, Cassandra brushed her fingers along the back of his hand. "I wish I could have met your dad," she said so softly he almost didn't hear it.

He looped his index finger around hers. "I do too," he whispered. Then, gave her a half-smirk. "But you'll get to meet Mom on the video call tomorrow, and she's pretty amazing."

Cassandra pressed her lips together. "Can I be honest?"

"Of course."

"I'm scared of meeting your mom."

Spencer laughed. "My mom is literally the least intimidating person in the world."

"I'm dating her baby," Cassandra objected. "She's going to think I'm some weird cradle robber, or gold digger, or something."

"You're not that much older than me."

"No, but she's your mom. Won't she be crazy protective of you?"

Spencer tipped his head to the side. "Honestly? She's probably just so thrilled that one of us is in a serious relationship at this point. She regularly complains about not having grandchildren." The moment the words were out of his mouth, he grimaced internally. Would Cassandra think he was suggesting they should have kids right away?

Evidently, the internal grimace made it to his face.

Cassandra nudged his elbow with hers. "Don't get weird on me now," she teased. "We did agree to assume we're going to stay together, right?"

He gave her a dry grin. "Right."

The doorbell rang then, saving them from any further awkwardness.

Cassandra jumped up from her seat, and Spencer followed. Her parents were already headed for the door. Waiting at the back of the hall, Spencer watched as they greeted their son and his family. Isaac Clement was the perfect blend of his parents, the resemblance to his sister plain too. He shared their dark, wavy hair, the arched Sauveterre brow, and sharp features. However, he bore his mother's longer, oval face, whereas Cassandra had her father's squared-off shape.

A jumble of excited greetings filled the air, the squeals of young children cutting through. Julianne immediately swept a toddler into her arms, his brown mop of hair sticking up funnily on the top. A pretty woman around Peter's age hugged Allen before handing the baby in her arms over to him for snuggles. Spencer had never been good at guessing kids' ages, and he didn't bother attempting it now.

A tremor of concern worked its way into Spencer's gut. He'd tried to tell himself he could handle meeting Cassandra's family. And after last night, he'd thought he'd be fine. But meeting her brother, his wife, and his kids, Spencer was beginning to question himself. If he were Peter, this would be no big deal. But Spencer was the reserved one. He was known explicitly for *not* being a people person. Yet here he was, desperate to make a good impression.

As the crowd of Clements began their way from the entry to where Cassandra and Spencer stood, Peter came clambering down the stairs. His hair was a mess, and he was still pulling his flannel on over his Henley as he skipped the final two steps. He skidded to a stop only inches from Spencer's side. "Sorry," he muttered. "I didn't want to be late."

Spencer gave him a disapproving look while Cassandra grinned and motioned for Peter to fix his collar. Then she turned to greet her brother. "Hi, Ike," she said fondly.

"We've missed you, Cassie," Isaac said, wrapping her up in a warm embrace. "Especially Timmy."

As if to prove his father's point, the toddler reached out from his grandma's arms, exclaiming, "Cassie!" Though with his toddler's lisp, it sounded more like "Caffie."

Cassandra smiled brightly, scooping the little boy from Julianne's arms. He giggled as she pretended to munch on his neck. "You're getting so big, Nutkin," she told him.

He mumbled something cute-sounding, holding up three fingers.

"Yes, I know," Cassandra said. "I was at your birthday party."

Everyone chuckled, smiling awkwardly at one another, waiting for the introductions to take place.

Cassandra hefted her nephew, Timmy, higher on her hip. "Uh, Ike, Sandy," she gestured behind her, "this is my boyfriend, Spencer, and his brother, Peter."

Isaac reached out to shake their hands in turn, and then Sandy did the same. She had warm brown hair, pretty blue eyes, and a sweetness to her smile that hinted at a friendly personality. Both Isaac and Sandy wore knit sweaters, his in a light brown and hers in a cheery cranberry.

Julianne nudged them further into the house, insisting they all take a seat in the living room while she finished up with breakfast. "Do you want coffee?" she asked. "Isaac, Sandy? Peter?"

They all said yes, and Peter added, "I'll help you get it."

Spencer slipped back into the kitchen for only a second to grab his and Cassandra's mugs before following the rest of the family into the living room. Timmy had insisted that Cassandra take him to the tree so he could show her his favorite ornaments (or at least, that's what Spencer assumed because the boy was now tottering around, tugging on Cassandra's arm as he pointed from one ornament to the next), so he took a seat on the couch.

Sandy helped Allen put his and Julianne's devotional supplies away before they sat on the loveseat with the baby. Isaac watched it all with a smile from the far side of the couch. Then he turned to Spencer. Something in his gaze shuttered, and it seemed as though his smile slipped as he cleared his throat. And thus came the second uncomfortable moment of the day.

"I can't remember if Cassandra told me your last name," Isaac prompted.

Spencer hesitated, still getting used to the new answer. "Varon," he said.

Isaac tipped his head to the side. "That sounds familiar. Dad," he turned to Allen, "do we know any Varons?"

Allen looked up from the baby on his lap. His eyes drifted to Spencer for a second before shaking his head. "They're an old family from DeVerre, but no, we don't know any personally."

"Hm." Isaac shifted in his seat. "And you're a writer?"

"I am."

"Anything I'd know?"

"Probably not," Spencer admitted, remembering Allen had said Isaac liked to read. "But I can give you the web address if you'd like to check out the blog. It's a historical paranormal mystery."

Peter then appeared, handing Sandy her mug of coffee before delivering the other to Isaac. "Julie told me how you like it, so let me know if you need more or less of anything," he said, then added, "She also told me to call her Julie, in case that weirded you out as much as it did me."

Sandy laughed lightly. "I felt the same when Isaac first brought me," she said. "But we're all family here."

"Not quite," Isaac said flatly. Then, he gave Spencer a false smile. "So, how do you like Washington? The cold getting to you?"

Noting the underhanded quip, Spencer shared a knowing glance with Peter just before his brother returned to the kitchen for his own coffee. "It's definitely different than Virginia," Spencer told Isaac. "But we're getting acclimated. And DeVerre has already become home."

"I don't know how you can stand such a tiny town," Isaac said, turning toward the tree. "I ask Cass every time she comes back: Why would you want to live in the backwoods when you've got the falls, Riverfront, and amazing restaurants here in Spokane?"

Cassandra sent her brother an annoyed look while she and Timmy returned, the little boy holding her fingers as they walked.

Spencer scooted to the side to make room for her beside him. "DeVerre is small, sure," he said. "But it sort of gets in your system. Once you move there, it won't let you go."

When Cassandra was seated, she helped Timmy up, who promptly sat himself down in her lap. "Caffie," he said, snuggling up and pointing at Spencer, "who's that?"

"That's Spencer," she told him.

"Who's he?"

"My boyfriend."

"Wha's that?"

Peter popped his head back in, announcing breakfast, saving Cassandra from having to come up with an answer.

Excitedly, Timmy jumped down, tugging on Cassandra's hand once again.

"Tim," Sandy called as she stood. She gave her son a firm look. "Don't pull on your aunt."

Timmy gave one last tug, then released Cassandra. "Sorry, Caffie," he mumbled.

"That's okay, Timmy." Cassandra stood beside Spencer. "Why don't you go save us a seat?"

With that, Timmy took off down the hall for the dining room.

Cassandra gave Spencer an amused grin. "He's kind of attached to me," she whispered.

"I can tell," Spencer replied, following the others down the hall. "I didn't realize you were around enough for that."

"Well, I used to visit regularly when he was really little, and then when Neil was born last year, I came down to watch Timothy for a few weeks while Sandy was recovering. With that and my month in Spokane after Mom's accident . . ." She shrugged. "He says I'm his best friend."

Spencer couldn't help his smile. "That's pretty adorable."

"What can I say? I'm good with kids." She grinned teasingly at him. "It's one of my most attractive traits."

When they rounded the corner into the dining room, they found Julianne and Peter filling the table with platters and bowls of food. They'd added more chairs to the table and a highchair off to the side where Allen was fastening Neil in behind the tray. Sandy took the seat beside him, pulling a plastic baggie of fruity cereal from a diaper bag.

Timmy was already seated in the middle of the table, calling Cassandra to sit next to him, presenting the third complication of the morning. With Allen at the head of the table and Isaac already seated across from him, Timmy's chosen seat left Cassandra, Spencer, and Peter to all split up throughout the table.

"Timothy," Sandy said, patting the empty chair beside her. "Come sit with me."

Timmy shook his head, pointing at Cassandra. "No. Caffie."

"Tim," Isaac warned. "Listen to your mother."

The boy scrunched his face determinedly. "I wanta sit with Caffie."

Seeing the impending meltdown, Spencer decided to be the hero in the moment. "That's okay," he said. "He can sit between us."

"Yeah," Peter jumped in. "That works great, actually. You can give me the cinnamon roll recipe while we eat, Julie."

"No," Isaac interjected, stopping them from taking their seats. He gave his son a pointed look. "He needs to learn to obey when he's given instructions."

Timmy looked about to burst into tears.

"We really don't mind," Spencer promised.

Isaac opened his mouth, ready to stand by his word, but Sandy set her hand on his wrist. She gave him a pleading look. "It's Christmas, baby," she said. "Let him sit with Cassie."

Backing down, Isaac nodded.

They took their seats and held hands during the prayer. Timmy all but ignored Spencer in favor of Cassandra at his side. He didn't mind exactly, as it gave him more time to talk with Allen and Julianne, seated across from him. But it created an additional barrier to him getting to know Isaac and Sandy, which he thought might be important, as Isaac seemed to take issue with Spencer's very presence.

Perhaps it was a protective older brother trait, but something told Spencer it had more to do with the fact that he wasn't Jacob—Isaac's best friend.

Even Peter was having better luck connecting with Isaac, seated by Sandy. They'd started talking about books and movies, smiling and laughing at their shared interests. Meanwhile, Spencer listened as Julianne explained that her family never celebrated Christmas or other holidays as anything more than passing days off, which led her to embrace the holiday spirit with everything she had as she grew older.

By the time breakfast was over, Spencer felt as though he and Cassandra had sat at opposite tables.

Julianne rose to begin gathering the remnants of the meal, and Spencer jumped up to help, collecting the dirty dishes. "Oh, that's all right," Isaac cut in when Spencer offered to take his plate. "I always help Mom with the dishes. Feel free to take a load off."

Spencer heard the dismissive inflection in his tone but didn't know how to reject the suggestion politely. Instead, he handed Isaac the remaining plates and stepped aside.

Timmy had already begun dragging Cassandra toward the living room, chanting, "Presents! Presents! Presents!" So, Spencer looked over at Peter at a loss.

Peter could only offer a shrug.

While Julianne and Isaac moved into the kitchen, Sandy went to the living room with baby Neil, and Allen began gathering the remaining breakfast leftovers.

Spencer stepped forward. "Why don't you let me help with that, Allen?" he said.

"You really don't have to, Spencer," he said knowingly. "We're your hosts. You can go take a seat, and we'll take care of the mess."

"I'd like to help," Spencer insisted.

Allen paused, then glanced at Peter. "You two aren't very good at taking no for an answer, are you?" he asked good-naturedly. Then he smiled. "All right. Julie could use help putting the food away while she and Ike do the dishes. Pete, do you know how to make a fire?"

Peter blinked. "Like, a campfire?"

"Like, a fire in the fireplace," Allen replied.

"Oh." Peter shrugged. "Yeah."

"Great. Why don't you do that? I'll get the gifts sorted."

Spencer picked up the tray of cinnamon rolls, the plate of sausages, and the bowl of fruit while the other men went off to their tasks. He headed into the kitchen, ready to ask Julianne where they kept their storage containers. Instead, he hesitated, hearing Isaac muttering, "I don't need a stranger undermining my authority as a father."

Spencer didn't intend to eavesdrop, but he didn't know what to say as Julianne smacked her son's arm with a dishtowel. "Nonsense," she said in a hushed tone. "He was trying to *help* you, Isaac."

"He was trying to make himself look good," he shot back.

"What a horrible thing to say," she said flatly. "You hardly know him."

While Spencer opened his mouth, ready to announce his presence, Isaac kept talking. "I don't want to know him. He isn't supposed to be here."

"Because he isn't Jacob?"

"Exactly."

Julianne shook her head. "He makes your sister happy," she said sharply. "Which is more than any of us have been able to say."

Spencer's gut twisted. He shouldn't have overheard this conversation, but he couldn't deny that he was glad he had. It was so clear; Allen and Julianne truly loved Cassandra, and they wanted to prove it even though they weren't entirely certain how to.

Wary of getting caught listening in, Spencer spoke up before Isaac could formulate a response. "Hey, Julie?"

The two of them spun, eyes wide as though caught in the act.

Which, Spencer thought wryly, they had been.

Hurrying on to make it seem like he overlooked their awkwardness, he said, "Allen told me to ask about where I could find storage containers for the leftovers."

"Oh." Julianne blinked a couple of times before smiling nervously. "Yes, yes, uh—they're in the cabinet above the toaster."

"Thanks." Spencer went about his task, pretending he'd never heard that Isaac wished he were Jacob or that Julianne had argued on his behalf. He found the perfectly sized glass containers for each food item and carefully placed them in the fridge. He double checked to see if they needed any more help, then headed into the living room when Julianne said no.

Spencer found Cassandra on the couch once more, but this time Peter held Timmy's attention, attempting to juggle some plastic ornaments for the kid's entertainment.

Taking the empty seat at Cassandra's side, Spencer smiled over at her. She scooted closer as if on instinct. "I'm sorry," she whispered.

"For what?" he replied quietly.

Her eyes glimmered apologetically. "For Ike."

Though he knew she couldn't be aware of the conversation he'd overheard, Spencer shook his head. "He's just loyal to his best friend," he said. "I can't fault him for that."

"I can," she grumbled.

Spencer brushed her arm, then slipped his fingers through hers. "Don't," he said. "He'll come around."

"Aren't you the optimist?" she said doubtfully.

Spencer chuckled. "Not especially. I can just see how much he cares about you," he said, then squeezed her hand. "Eventually, he'll see that I do too. And when he does, then it won't matter that I'm not his best friend. He'll be happy because you're happy. Because he loves you."

Spencer almost added, "and I do too," but kept his tongue in check.

It wasn't time for that yet.

However, Cassandra stared at him with parted lips. Her gaze softened. "You're really cute," she whispered.

Spencer couldn't contain the grin that split across his face. "I'd say thank you," he teased, "but you're the one who said I look like I decided to ignore basic hygiene earlier."

"I did not," she retorted, jabbing a finger into his side.

Spencer laughed, wrapping his arm around her shoulder. He didn't bother with a witty quip. He just held her close, pleased to be with Cassandra in her family's house. And despite all the awkwardness of this first introduction, he hoped it wouldn't be their last visit.

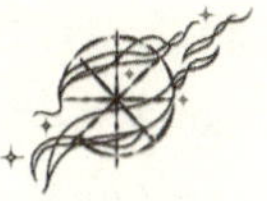

CHAPTER FOURTEEN

Cassandra

Sitting on the couch between Spencer and Peter as they opened gifts with her family, Cassandra found herself awed by the revelation that she was having fun. In Spokane. With her *family*.

Cassandra tugged at the ribbon on the gift her dad had just handed her. They were taking turns, enjoying watching each other open what they'd received from their Christmas lists. Even though Cassandra hadn't intended to join for the holiday, she had bought them gifts, planning to send them in the mail. Now, she was glad she hadn't.

On the floor, Timmy was already playing with the gift she and Spencer had gotten for him together. The icebreaker of the gift had the toddler readily talking with Spencer, and suddenly, *he* was the boy's best friend instead of Cassandra.

Peter and Spencer had insisted on bringing a gift for Cassandra's parents too. Which turned out to be a good idea because Allen, who played Santa during the gift-giving, handed out gifts sans costume, placing a package in each Spencer's and Peter's hands.

Though she didn't want to admit it, it seemed to Cassandra that her parents really were trying. A fact that made her stomach squirm and her emotions fray. After all this time, were they suddenly going to love her despite her choice to leave them?

When they'd opened their stockings, Cassandra had found a small envelope among the trinkets and candy. The flourish on the C of her name told her that it was her mother who'd placed it there. They'd never exchanged cards in the Clement house, not even for birthdays. Words were said aloud rather than in writing. So, this letter struck Cassandra with its peculiarity, and she tucked it away, unsure if she would ever read it.

After gifts were exchanged, Cassandra and the brothers gathered their things, preparing to leave. Peter offered to take their bags to the Jeep, leaving Spencer and Cassandra to face her family in the hall. Timmy was still dogging Spencer's steps, reminding Cassandra of Nex, while Julianne pressed a paper bag filled with cookies and some baked goods into his hand.

Isaac put an arm around Cassandra's shoulders, drawing her back from the others just enough to whisper, "Tell me, Andy: what is it about this guy?"

Looking up at her brother, Cassandra could see that there was no spite in his tone, only open curiosity.

She smiled, nudging his side with her elbow. "He's different," she said. "He's kind, and he's strong. He's compassionate and thoughtful and, admittedly, weird. But in the best way."

Isaac's dark gaze held hers questioningly.

"I know you just met him," she said, "but give him a chance. I think he'll surprise you."

Though Isaac didn't say anything to agree, he gave her a nod and a squeeze. "I miss having you here, Cass," he said but didn't pressure her any further.

In fact, none of her family had pushed for her return to Spokane. Aside from Isaac's earlier disparagement of DeVerre, there hadn't been a single underhanded comment about Cassandra moving back. Which was, in truth, a great shock. Her parents *always* made pointed remarks about what she was missing out on, or how family was meant to be close, or that she was hurting them by rejecting their love.

Cassandra chewed on the inside of her lip as she gave Sandy and the boys hugs. The Clements were trying. And wasn't that what she'd always wished for from them? That, even if they didn't understand, they would *try* to love her as she was.

Peter and Spencer shook hands with Allen, and then Julianne pulled each of them in for a gentle hug. "You're welcome back anytime," she told them both.

It was Cassandra's turn to hug Allen then. Cautiously, her dad wrapped his arms around her as though she'd break if he held on too tight. "Thank you for coming, sweetheart," he said.

Heart pinching with a blend of anxiety, hurt, and hope, Cassandra returned the hug. "Thanks for having us," she forced herself to say.

Allen pulled back, hands still on her arms as he lowered his voice. "I like him," he said, his stare adamantly holding hers. "He seems like a good fit for you."

Cassandra glanced over his shoulder to where Spencer was shaking hands with Isaac in farewell. She smiled as he gave Timmy a high five.

Turning back to her dad, Cassandra couldn't help but smile. "He is," she promised.

Allen dipped his chin in an approving nod, then stepped back. Julianne waited there, her crystal-blue eyes locked on Cassandra's face. She approached nervously and gave her a hug that could only be called timid.

When she pulled back, Julianne locked gazes with her, the scars reminding Cassandra of what the Druids had done to their family. For years, Julianne and Allen had chosen to lie to her, placing pressure on her and being unsupportive, believing it was for her own good. And

Cassandra had chosen to ignore their desires, drawing the wrath of the Druids upon her mom.

It wasn't Cassandra's fault. She was learning to accept that truth. But she still couldn't help feeling the weight of her choices.

Julianne gave a weak smile, taking a step back. "Merry Christmas, Cassie," she said with no more expectation in her words than simple love.

Cassandra couldn't find her full voice enough to return the words in more than a whisper. Then, she turned and walked out the door with Spencer and Peter. She got in the Jeep, not bothering to look back at the house. She couldn't with the strange swell of emotion rolling through her chest.

After years of feeling like nothing she did was ever good enough, Cassandra blinked at the road ahead, wondering at the past day's experience. Things weren't fixed. Her relationship with her family was still awkward and shaky at best. But after all this time, Cassandra would take this hope, this knowledge that they were trying to be happy for her, even if that meant she wasn't with them.

Turning in her seat, Cassandra looked over at Spencer and then at Peter in the back seat. "Thanks for coming with me," she said. "You didn't have to do this, but . . ."

"We were happy to," Spencer said, taking her hand without hesitation.

Peter gave her one of his dry grins, a knowing gleam in his eyes. "It wasn't much of a chore for me," he said. "They aren't *my* girlfriend's family. While Spence had to be on his best behavior, I got to kick back and watch the chaos unfold."

"It wasn't that bad," Spencer said. "Your dad is actually kind of cool."

Cassandra scoffed. "He's an accountant. They could never be considered 'cool.'"

Spencer smirked. "He reminds me of you."

Ignoring the sneaky compliment, Cassandra eyed him warily. "How so?"

"He's no-nonsense, clever, and he sees through people's crap."

Spencer gave her one of his more teasing looks. "He's also secretly a softie."

Cassandra rolled her eyes as Peter snorted in the backseat.

The rest of the drive back to DeVerre was filled with light chatter and talk about the rest of their vacation. They ignored the work that awaited them on the other side of the holiday weekend. They didn't talk about the Spectral attached to Cassandra, or when it might surface at last. They didn't discuss finding Anna or how they might resurrect her. There was no mention of Druids, the Warden, or the spirit world.

It was as though they'd agreed that during their drive, they could be other people. Not Varons, not a Vessel. Just three friends who were enjoying the holiday together.

When they got back to Occasus, the sky was dimming to a muted blue-gray. After their large breakfast, they hadn't been hungry for lunch, only snacking as they opened gifts. But when they walked into the house, its halls were filled with a warm, cheesy, and potato-y scent, and they all perked up excitedly.

Connor sat on the couch, *It's a Wonderful Life* on in the background while he wrote in a notebook. Anguis and Nex lounged at his feet until they entered the room. "Hey," he said as the dogs raced over in greeting. "How was it?"

"It was good," Cassandra said, eyeing the scene before her. A plate with cookie crumbles sat on the coffee table, a small, wrapped gift sitting next to it. It appeared that Connor had gotten into the Christmas spirit at last.

"What's going on here?" Peter asked.

"Hm? Oh." Connor looked at the wrapping supplies around him. He ripped a piece of paper out of the notebook. "I was just getting Josiah's Christmas gift together."

"That's nice of you," Cassandra said.

Connor nodded. "It was only right. I'm going to adopt him, so I think it's best if I start acting like a dad. Or something like that, at least."

Cassandra, Spencer, and Peter gaped at him.

"You're gonna . . . what?" Peter asked incredulously.

Connor looked up at them, nonplussed. "I've decided to adopt him. Of course, I can't really do that until I'm done with medical school, but I've planned it all out." He waved the notebook paper at them. "Once I graduate, I'll return here and buy a house. I know the Warden wants him to be part of a family with a mom and a dad, so once we resurrect Anna, I'll marry her, and we can adopt Josiah together."

Though Cassandra didn't think Anna would object to any of that, she exchanged a glance with Peter and Spencer, who both looked to be holding back laughter.

"That's pretty thorough planning, Zeus," Peter teased.

"It's enough to convince Rhader," Connor said matter-of-factly. "Once I get him to agree, I'll figure out the rest of the details."

Cassandra pressed her lips together, knowing that one of those details was secretly taken care of for him already. To deflect, she gestured toward the kitchen. "Do I smell soup?" she asked.

"Oh, yeah." Connor folded up the paper and grabbed Josiah's gift from the table. "I put some cheesy corn chowder in the slow cooker. It's one of Aimee's old recipes. They make it every Christmas Eve."

"Okay, Mr. Mom," Peter said, eying Connor amusedly. "Who are you and what've you done with our grumpy roommate?"

Connor grinned. "I decided he was boring," he said. "I thought it'd be better to be the man Anna loved instead."

Cassandra had the inexplicable urge to coo, "aww." Instead, she scrunched her nose at the overtly feminine compulsion and grabbed her bag from Spencer. "I'm going to unpack," she said, then smiled at the reformed Druid. "Merry Christmas, Connor."

Anguis darted up the stairs ahead of Cassandra as though preparing the way to her room. He wagged his tail, waiting for her at the top. She shifted the bag of presents further onto her arm as she reached out to scratch his ear.

In her room, she set the canvas bag and her duffel on the bed. She decided to distribute the gifts first, as they were the most exciting to unpack. She placed the two new books Isaac and Sandy had given her on the short bookshelf by the fireplace, then returned for the rest of the gifts from her parents. As she sorted through her things, the corner of the letter from her mom poked her finger.

Cassandra stared at it, lips pursed. She didn't want to read it. She was inherently adverse to anything her mother had written. It was likely another attempt to play on her sympathies. They'd probably kept quiet all weekend simply because Spencer was there. Now, this card was meant to undercut their goodwill and guilt Cassandra into coming home.

Rolling her eyes at herself, Cassandra picked up the card. She was being ridiculous. If it was anything more than a simple Christmas card, she could stop reading it. She'd skim the letter at the most. And who knew, it could even have a gift card inside.

Cassandra ripped open the back flap. There was no gift card or cash inside; simply a folded sheet of paper with Julianne's handwriting.

Her heart pricked. So, this was a letter meant to manipulate her.

Dispassionately, Cassandra scanned the first lines, ready to toss the letter in the trash the moment she read the first disparaging word.

Then, she sat down on her bed and read the whole thing.

Cassandra,

I hope you read this letter. I know there's a chance you'll throw it out, but I didn't know how else to tell you this.

I'm sorry, sweetheart. For everything. There may be a day when I can say that out loud to you, but for now, this will have to be enough.

I've never been good with words. I've never been good with you. And I'm sorry for that.

There is no explanation for why I did what I did through the years, but my fear. My family raised me to be a Druid. When I was a girl, I never liked their tenants or dogma. It always felt wrong to me, but it was who my parents were, who they wanted me to be. When I went to college and met your father, I learned that Druidism truly was wrong. Yet, I couldn't abandon my family. I couldn't leave Debbie. She was my sister more than my cousin. We did everything together. We dreamed of raising our families together.

When we married, I asked your father if we could live in DeVerre, and he said yes. We moved there and began our family. And we were so very happy. Then you started seeing ghosts.

I knew the moment we learned of it that the Druids would want you. The very life I had hoped to protect you from had found you.

I cannot defend my actions from there. I can only say that as your mother, I feared losing you to them. I was of no consequence; I had never displayed great power, so they let me live free of their influence. But I knew, no matter their acceptance of my separation, they would demand a Wielder as powerful as you join them.

So, we ran away. And ever since, you fought me. I was trying to keep you safe, but you rejected my protection. You aren't a mother yet, so you may not be able to understand, but that hurt me. It felt like you were rejecting me. I feared what they would do if you discovered the truth. I feared that they would corrupt you and turn you to their cause. Worse, I feared that they would kill you if you refused.

I realize now that I was wrong about everything.

I don't expect you to believe me. I don't expect you to forgive me. But I want you to know, my sweet girl, I love you, and if I could go back in time, I would tell you the truth. I would have let you understand what I was protecting you from. Then maybe you would have felt loved rather than stifled. Because I do love you, Cassandra. I always will.

I won't ask you to return my love or to visit us in Spokane. I only ask that you forgive me if you can.

Merry Christmas,

Mom

Cassandra didn't realize she was crying until the first tear hit the page. Then, she heard a knock on her still-open door. "Cass?" Spencer's voice carried to her.

She tossed the letter aside and wiped at her face, turning to him. "Hey, uh—what, uh . . . ?"

Spencer stared at her in shock, stepping into the room. "Are you okay?"

"Yeah, I'm—I'm fine," she insisted. "My mom . . ."

"What'd she do?" he asked, a hint of defensiveness in his tone.

Cassandra motioned toward the double-sided letter but found she couldn't speak through the tears in her throat. So she grabbed the paper and handed it to Spencer. He eyed her carefully before reading it too.

When he was done, he folded it back up and met her gaze questioningly.

Cassandra still couldn't speak, so she just nodded.

Spencer returned the nod, set the letter back down, then pulled her into a hug.

Tucking her chin, Cassandra buried her face in Spencer's neck. Her heart was broken. Sorrow for the past twenty-five years flowed out of her as she cried silently in his arms. She lamented the loss of what could have been if her mother had taught Cassandra about the spirit world, the Druids, and the reason they'd had to leave DeVerre. She mourned the pain she'd endured because of Julianne's fear. She regretted the hurt she'd caused her mom because she didn't understand the woman's faulty attempt at protection. And most of all, she grieved the loss of Diane, her mother's accident, and all the death the Druids had caused because she hadn't known the truth.

Cassandra didn't know when she would feel ready to forgive her mom or her dad. Even with how hard they were trying, even with this apology, it still didn't feel like enough. But she hoped that maybe one day it would be.

~

Hours later, after her tears had dried and they'd talked through the letter, Cassandra and Spencer entered DeVerre Chapel with Peter and Connor. The sanctuary was decorated with pine branches and velvet ribbons, candles and sparkling stars, nativity sets and poinsettias. Nearly every DeVerrean was there to celebrate Christmas.

Joining the Lamberts, the four of them took their seats after much greeting and well-wishing. They were well known now. People regularly stopped them to thank them for saving the town. The new Warden members sought their approval. It was a side-effect, Cassandra thought, of being Varons and the people closest to them.

On their way forward, Connor found the Calderons and invited Josiah to sit with them. The little boy practically beamed with joy.

For the next couple of hours, they sang carols, listened to Sam's sermon, lit candles, had communion, and contemplated the greatest gift ever given.

Then, they returned to Occasus under the blanket of a fresh snowfall.

"All right," Peter said, hurrying to the stairs. "Time for some eggnog and—"

A chunk of white powder slammed into his back.

Cassandra peered around the car, unable to tell if it was Spencer or Connor who'd thrown the snowball. By the amused looks on their faces, it could have been either.

Slowly, Peter turned around, surveying them all. Evidently, he was as unable to deduce the culprit as Cassandra. "What are you, twelve?" he said to the men.

Connor smirked, and Spencer shrugged. "A snowball fight was on the list," his brother said, confessing to the crime.

Peter frowned. "No, it wasn't."

"It was on *our* list," Cassandra offered.

"Then, why don't you two have a snowball fight?" Peter sniped.

Another snowball hit Peter on the chest, nicking his chin in the process.

Connor sniggered, the assailant this time.

"That's it!" Peter said, then scooped a handful of snow off the porch railing. He lobbed it at Spencer. And all-out war erupted across the lawn.

Heaps of snow flew through the air, the four of them laughing and chasing each other around. None of them cared that they were adults, too old for such antics. Cassandra took a snowball to the shoulder, then heaved another at Peter's face. Joy bubbled out of her as Spencer snuck up behind her and pinned her arms, making her an easy target.

After months of pain, loss, and death, Cassandra needed this. She needed the freedom to squeal in protest as another snowball exploded against her coat. The release of laughter doubled her over as she kicked out, driving both her and Spencer back into the snow.

They landed with an "oof," and his arms loosened.

"You okay?" Connor asked, the snowball fire ceasing.

Cassandra and Spencer caught their breath and began to laugh.

Peter snorted. "They're fine." He slapped Connor's arm. "I'd say we won. How about we celebrate with some 'nog?"

"I'll drink to that," Connor said.

Sitting up beside her, Spencer reined in his laughter. "Go on," he said with a wave of his hand. "We'll be right there."

"It's freezing out here," Peter noted, but Spencer threw a fistful of snow at him, and he retreated. "Don't catch a cold," he ordered just before going inside.

Cassandra looked at Spencer, her butt growing numb despite the protection of her coat. "What are we still doing out here?" she asked.

"There's still one more thing on our list," he said.

She furrowed her brow, trying to remember. Then, Spencer gave her shoulder a shove and flopped onto his back, going spread-eagled.

"Snow angels," Cassandra remarked drolly. "Seriously?"

Waving his arms and legs through the snow, Spencer grinned. "You're the one who suggested it."

Shaking her head, Cassandra accepted the silly romantic gesture for what it was. She settled herself down on the snow far enough from Spencer's side to create her own snow angel. Her nose tingled by the time she was done, and her coat was almost soaked through. But as Spencer helped her up to survey their winter art, her heart felt fuller than it had in a long time.

Spencer settled his arm over her shoulders. "Well," he said appraisingly, "I'd say we've done fine work here."

She chuckled and jabbed his ribs. Then she slipped her arms around his waist. "You know," she said, looking into his icy blue gaze, "you're a sap."

His smile crinkled the corners of his eyes. "Only for you," he said.

"That's a good line."

"Thanks." He turned, wrapping his other arm around her. "But I've got a better one."

"Oh, yeah?" She snuggled closer. "Are you gonna tell me I make the prettiest snow angel in the entire universe?"

"No."

"Or is it that I'm the best crafter you've ever met?"

"Definitely not that."

She bit her lip to keep from laughing. "What else could you possibly have to say?"

Spencer's gaze softened, and even through her coat, she could feel his thumbs brush along her back as he said, "I love you."

Cassandra stilled.

She blinked.

She couldn't have heard him correctly.

Spencer held her befuddled stare patiently as his words sank in.

"You love me?" she whispered.

Spencer nodded, silent.

Breath caught in her lungs, Cassandra teared up for the second time that day. There were so many arguments in her head that told her it couldn't be true. He hadn't known her long enough. They hadn't been dating long enough. He only thought he loved her because they'd gone through so much over the last two months. The holiday was giving him rosy feelings, and he'd regret his words in the morning.

But in Spencer's steady gaze, Cassandra didn't see a single bit of hesitation or uncertainty. That was the thing about the Varon brothers. They didn't care by half measures. They gave their whole being to the people around them. It was obvious to see in the way Peter behaved. It was harder to catch in Spencer's more reserved nature. But he was telling the truth. He loved her.

"Spencer . . ." His name came out in a foggy breath that swirled between them.

"Yeah?" he whispered back.

"I love you too."

He smiled and settled his forehead against hers. His gloved hand came up to cup her cheek, the fabric still slightly damp from the snow. Cassandra didn't care. She leaned in, blissfully happy to know that she was loved by the man she longed to call home.

CHAPTER FIFTEEN

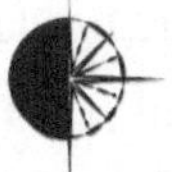

Spencer

Christmas morning came with an overcast, gray sky. It should have felt dreary, but instead, there was a new magic in the air as Spencer pulled on a sweater and jeans. He was under no illusions that it was thanks to his and Cassandra's love confession the previous night . . . or the following, extended kisses that lasted until they were both sniffling from the cold.

This was, without a doubt, the best Christmas he'd had since he could remember.

Hurrying downstairs with Nex at his side, Spencer found the rest of the house asleep. He set a pot of coffee brewing, then set to work on breakfast. They'd agreed to sleep in, but he knew that the smell of bacon and French toast would be enough to draw the others out.

He was right.

Within an hour, the brothers, Cassandra, and Connor sat in the living room, munching on their breakfast as they enjoyed their languid morning. Once their plates were empty, Peter didn't waste any time getting the presents out from under the tree.

"Here ya go, boys," he said, handing Anguis and Nex their new bones, each wrapped with a shiny blue ribbon. "These are from your parents, not me. I didn't get you anything."

The dogs took the bones and turned their backs on him to enjoy their gifts in peace.

The fire crackled as Cassandra handed Spencer and Peter their presents.

"Why does Spence get two gifts?" Peter teased.

"Because he's my boyfriend," she replied, tucking her feet under her as she sat next to Spencer once again.

Spencer pulled the wrapping off the first gift, which was clearly a book by its shape. A smart purchase, he thought. It was a fantasy novel that he vaguely remembered mentioning in passing. The second gift was a leather keychain loop with an embossed note. *"Frankly, I'd slay every monster to get to you. xo, Serene."*

Spencer held up the keychain, smirking at Cassandra. "Did you plagiarize my work?" he teased.

Cassandra nodded smugly. "I most certainly did. Though I don't mean it sarcastically."

Remembering the scene from *Wenzely & Frankly*, Spencer chuckled. "Neither did Serene," he said. "Frankly's just too dense to know the difference between sarcasm and flirting."

Peter opened his gift next, tossing the wrapping paper to the floor. Connor eyed it disapprovingly, then excused himself to get a trash bag. "He's already such a good dad," Peter commented, then opened the box and pulled out a notebook.

Spencer smiled, knowing that the bottom right corner was embossed with the Varon crest. Cassandra had asked him if he thought it was a good idea, and he did, in fact, think it was a great idea. Though Peter was struggling to accept the new role of true Varon, Spencer knew even something as small as this would make him feel more qualified for the task.

With a sly smile, Peter thanked Cassandra, clearly happy with the gift. "It's a good thing too," he said. "I've almost filled my last notebook."

"That's what gave me the idea," she said.

Spencer gathered his gifts, and Peter jumped up to do the same. They handed them out, leaving one gift on the coffee table while Connor returned with the trash bag. He began picking up wrapping paper as they finished their gift-giving.

With an annoyed huff, Spencer lifted Peter's gift to him. "Seriously?"

Peter gave him a bland glare. "Your other one has a literal hole in the back left shoulder. I'm not letting you look like a bum any longer."

Refolding the new denim jacket, Spencer gave Cassandra an "I told you so" look.

She rolled her eyes. "I still say you look like a woodsman in that thing."

"Maybe if the woodsman is a homeless hermit," Peter said, then gestured toward Cassandra. "It's your turn."

"Open this first," Spencer instructed.

"Is it from you?" she asked.

"Yeah."

With a bright smile, Cassandra tore free the paper. Spencer watched as she pulled out the pack of highlighters first, grateful that he'd thought ahead and bought her two gifts too. "For my devotionals?" she asked, inspecting the gray gradient set.

Spencer nodded. "I thought you'd like the color."

She chuckled, then reached back into the box and removed the cream package with gold lettering on the front. Her lips parted in surprise as her dark eyes found his.

"I checked the one in your room," Spencer explained, motioning to the box of perfume. Then he blanched. "Not that I was snooping or anything—"

Cassandra reached over and kissed his cheek, silencing him. "I love it," she said. "It's just . . . This was Diane's perfume. I started wearing it because it reminded me of her."

Spencer didn't know how to feel about that. He'd never met Diane, so he supposed it shouldn't be weird, but he'd always attributed the scent to Cassandra. But he realized she'd like that. Cassandra's love for Diane was deep, and she would take whatever connection to the woman she could get.

"I'm glad you like it," Spencer said.

Cassandra squeezed his hand, a glimmer of tears in her eyes. She turned to Peter then. "Your turn," she instructed.

"You don't have to tell me twice," Peter said, then made a mess of the wrapping paper once more. "Oh, nice!"

Peter pulled out the bound collection of *Wenzel & Frankly's* serial episodes. Spencer had ordered it weeks ago, knowing that he wanted to give his brother a gift on Christmas, even if they didn't celebrate the holiday as they usually did. He'd even hired an artist to illustrate a scene from the books to put on the cover.

After oohing over the book for several minutes, noting all the details Spencer had made sure the illustrator put in the cover design, Peter finally picked up the second gift. "What's this?" he asked, holding up the small box.

"It's a tracking tag," Spencer said. "Put it in your shoe or whatever. I'm not losing you again."

They all laughed, but Peter's smile held a secretly pleased tilt that told Spencer he knew the true sentiment behind the joke.

"All right," Cassandra said, holding up the small gift she had left. She looked at Peter. "Is this one from you?"

"And Spence," Peter said. "But it was my idea, so you can consider it from me."

She chuckled, peeling back the paper. Her brow furrowed when she saw the fancy box within. With a glance at both Peter and Spencer, she finally lifted the cover. And her jaw went slack.

"As the true Varon," Peter said tenderly, "I think I'm officially allowed to induct people into the family."

Cassandra's eyes were full of tears as she lifted the small silver ring from the cushion inside.

Spencer smiled over at Peter, proud of his brother's idea. Right after the fight at the Veil, only a few days after Cassandra had removed her Sauveterre family crest for the final time, Peter had told Spencer of his idea. He wanted to replace the signet ring with one bearing the Varon family crest. A reminder that, no matter what, Cassandra would be part of their family from that day on. She'd saved their lives (numerous times), she'd given them their inheritance, and she'd made a permanent home in their hearts.

With a small sniffle, Cassandra slipped the ring onto her right pinky finger, exactly where the old one had resided. "That's, uh—" She wiped at her eyes with her free hand, gaze still locked on the signet. She sniffled again, then looked up at Peter and Spencer. "That's really nice," she said, then scrunched her face in a failing fight against the tears.

Spencer quickly pulled Cassandra close, kissing the top of her head. Peter shook his head at the emotional display, though he smiled brightly.

As Cassandra leaned into his side, brushing at her silent tears, Spencer tipped his chin up toward Peter. His brother got the signal and picked up the last gift from the coffee table.

"Mkay, final gift." Peter turned to Connor, in the middle of folding some tissue paper. "Merry Christmas, Zeus."

Connor paused, staring at the gift, then up at Peter. "What?"

"It's from all of us."

The man blinked. "Oh, I, uh—" Connor looked abashed. "I didn't even think to get you guys anything."

"We didn't expect you to," Spencer said.

"And it's pretty small," Peter said. He shook the box playfully. "How great can it be, right?"

Reluctantly, Connor took the box. He studied Peter, aware of his blatant sarcasm. "Thanks," he murmured, then pulled free the string.

Very carefully, Connor unwrapped the gift, making Spencer wonder if the Frossards opened their gifts with a letter opener. After folding the wrapping paper and putting it in the trash, Connor finally opened the box.

He stared for several seconds before lifting the pair of keys. "What's this?" he asked.

Peter shrugged casually. "Well, we couldn't wrap a house, so we just wrapped the keys."

Connor's brow furrowed intensely. "What are you talking about?"

"We got you and Anna a house," Peter said. "The places here in DeVerre are stupidly cheap. And the one next door to Aaron's was for sale, so we thought: Why the heck not? You can stay here in Occasus as long as you want, but any time you'd like, the place is yours."

"You bought me a house?"

"To be fair," Cassandra jumped in. "My job with the Warden isn't official yet, so I'm still broke. *They* bought you a house. I bought the keychain. Which wasn't a hassle since I bought Spence one too."

Connor rubbed his finger along the leather loop. Spencer knew Cassandra had ordered it with the embossing *"C+A, est. 2001."*

"I double-checked the year with Ava," Cassandra said.

Connor got a weird look on his face, his lips pursed, and his nose scrunched as he studiously avoided looking at any of them. "Thanks," he said again, his voice taut around barely restrained tears.

The three of them exchanged pleased grins. While Connor wasn't exactly in dire straits, the Frossard estate was locked in probate, and with his mother still alive, there was no telling how much money he'd get or when he'd get it. As a college student, he had little time for a job, so all his meager funds went straight to living day to day. They knew getting a home would be difficult. And now that Connor intended to adopt Josiah, the gift was even more meaningful.

To help distract from Connor's emotional state, Spencer reminded them that they were supposed to call their mom and stepdad soon. Cassandra hopped up first, muttering something about getting ready. Though she already had on makeup and Spencer thought she looked just fine, he knew she wanted to make a good impression on his mom, so he didn't stop her.

Peter and Spencer cleaned up and put away their new gifts. Connor disappeared up the stairs while they grabbed Spencer's laptop to set up the video call.

When Cassandra returned in one of her new sweaters, her hair freshly styled, they took a seat on one of the couches. Spencer settled the computer on his lap while Peter told her, "Remember, they don't know about the whole Varon thing yet."

Cassandra frowned. "It's been over a month," she said.

"Yeah, well . . ." Peter replied lamely.

"You need to fix that."

Spencer shared a look with Peter. "We know," he promised. Then he pulled up the video call.

After just a few rings, the excited face of Mallory Collins-Powell appeared on the screen. "Ahh!" she cried, her bright smile filling Spencer with joy. "Boys! Oh, you look so cute. Is that a new sweater, Petey?" Before any of them could actually respond beyond smiling, Mallory called to her husband, "Ben, the boys are on."

Mallory turned back to the camera. She looked just like she always had. Her long, brown hair hung in pretty waves, framing her oval face. She had the same deep-set brown eyes and narrow nose as Peter. She wore a bright red-and-white sweater and light makeup. She'd always been a natural beauty; Spencer's dad had said so regularly, and as he'd grown older, he'd come to realize it was true.

"Merry Christmas," Mallory said as she waited for Ben to join her. "Have you guys already opened your presents?"

"Yeah," Peter said, taking the lead. "We just finished a bit ago. How about you two?"

"No, no." Mallory waved a hand casually as Ben finally sat at her side. She patted his arm. "Ben's brother, Marcus, and his family are coming over later, and we'll do gifts then."

"Hey, guys," Ben cut in quickly. "Merry Christmas."

Spencer and Peter returned the greeting, Cassandra sitting at their side, smiling silently. Spencer had always liked Ben Powell. He'd been best friends with their Uncle Matthew—who was really their adoptive cousin, though they'd always called him "Uncle Matt"—and had joined them at many family get-togethers through the years. He was funny, friendly, and level-headed. He'd even been incredibly helpful after their dad's death, helping out whenever they needed work done on the house or hanging out with the brothers, taking them to ball games or concerts their mom didn't want to attend.

It hadn't been until Peter and Spencer were ready to move out that they'd decided enough was enough. Mallory had been a widow for over six years, and they didn't want their mom to live alone anymore. So, they'd begun the matchmaking process—or, rather, Peter had with Spencer's approval—and a year later, Mallory and Ben had married.

After their exchange of greetings, Peter elbowed Spencer.

Spencer elbowed him back to confirm that he knew. "Hey, uh—" Spencer interjected. "Mom, Ben, this is my girlfriend, Cassandra."

"Hi," Cassandra said with a timid wave.

Mallory's smile could have lit the living room of Occasus through the computer screen with its brightness. "I am *so* happy to meet you, Cassandra," she said enthusiastically. "The boys have both told me so much about you. I feel like we're friends already."

Cassandra's expression was between relieved and uncertain. "I'm delighted to meet you too," she said. "Spence and Pete talk about how amazing you are all the time."

Mallory blushed happily. "You are so perfect. Isn't she perfect?" she said to Ben.

Ben draped his arm over the back of Mallory's chair. "Fair warning,

Cassandra," he said jokingly, "you're the only thing Mal has talked about for the last month. Don't give her your number or she'll never leave you alone."

They all chuckled, and Mallory pinched his side. Then she turned back to the camera, smile as big as ever. "Oh, I wish we could be there!" she said. "I miss my boys."

"We miss you too, Mom. Maybe you could come next year," Spencer said.

Mallory looked at Ben for a moment. "Well, we were actually just talking about that," she said. "What would you guys think about me coming for Petey's birthday in the spring? I have a bunch of vacation time saved up at work, and I could come for a whole two weeks."

Though Spencer had meant for them to come for next Christmas, the suggestion sparked an idea in his mind. "Yeah!" he replied instantly. "I think that'd be great!"

Peter and Cassandra glanced at him in surprise.

Then Peter turned back to the camera. "Uh, yeah, we'd love that," he said. "But we'll have to check our schedule. You know," he gave Spencer a pointed look, "'cause we might have a friend visiting at that time. . . ."

At Peter's hint, Spencer remembered: While the Spectral hadn't made its appearance yet, the Warden said that it was often common. In fact, they said that frequently, with the initial release, the "rebirth" didn't happen until the spring equinox, which would be March 20 next year. With Peter's birthday on April 2, the Spectral's expected arrival was right before Mallory wanted to come.

"Oh, right." Spencer shrugged noncommittally. "We can talk about it."

But as they continued to talk with their mom and stepdad, Spencer wasn't sure he cared about the questionable timing. After all, Cassandra was right. They needed to tell their mom the truth about DeVerre and their Varon inheritance. They couldn't keep lying to her about the spirit world. And if Cassandra were going to carry this Spectral for the rest of her life, if her children would carry it as well, then Mallory would have to learn about that too.

As the conversation started to wrap up, Spencer made his decision. He'd had the idea in the past, but it had only been a fun daydream. Now that he and Cassandra were dating, now that they were in love, the idea was no longer purely theoretical. So, as they wound their way toward their goodbyes, Spencer spoke up.

"Uh, Mom, I just remembered," he interrupted. They all turned to him, and he felt his palms grow sweaty. "I wanted to ask you something before you go."

"Okay," Mallory said, then waited.

Spencer blinked. "Like, just you and me."

"Oh. Yeah, all right." Mallory gave her last goodbyes to Cassandra and Peter, as did Ben. Then Spencer hopped up from the couch.

Both Peter and Cassandra gave Spencer weird looks, but he waved them off. "Story idea," he lied.

Neither of them seemed to buy it, but he didn't particularly care.

Carrying the laptop up to his room, Spencer shut the door and climbed onto his bed. "Okay," he said, rubbing his hands together. "Sorry about that."

Ben had disappeared, just leaving Mallory behind to smile gently at him. "What is it, Squishy?" she asked.

Spencer ignored the childhood nickname. "So, I was wondering . . ." He paused, nervous. "I know it's fast and everything, but . . . I want to marry Cassandra."

Mallory's brow rose. "Oh, Spence." Her eyes teared up. "Baby, I'm so happy for you! She seems wonderful."

"She really is." Spencer forced himself to keep going. "I want to give it time, but I've been thinking that after a little bit—when I'm ready to propose . . . I'd like to use the ring Dad gave you. If that's okay?"

Mallory sniffled. "That's more than okay, baby." She wiped at her face. "I, uh—would you want me to bring it when I come in the spring?

Would that—would that be soon enough? Or—I don't really want to send it in the mail."

"No, no. When you come is fine." Spencer massaged his palm, feeling both excited and anxious. "Maybe you can help me plan it?"

Mallory pressed her hands to her mouth, unable to hide her huge grin. "I'd love to!"

Spencer returned her smile, his heart practically pounding out of his chest. He was going to propose to Cassandra. Be it several months from now, he was going to ask her to marry him. With all the impossibilities that had happened to him in the last two months—hellhounds, Druids, the spirit world, wielding, and Spectrals . . .

After all of that, the most wonderful impossibility of them all was Cassandra Clement. And he couldn't wait to spend the rest of his life with her.

Peter

The rest of Christmas day was spent relaxing and reading until late in the afternoon when Cassandra forced them up to get cooking. With the biggest house, Peter and Spencer had invited the Lambert and Bernard families to join them for dinner at Occasus.

While their guests would bring several dishes to the meal, they'd volunteered to provide the ham and mashed potatoes. So, they worked together, cooking, setting the table, and cleaning up for their company.

When they'd arrived, and the house was full of chatter, Peter smiled to himself. He carved the ham with Spencer at his side, holding the plate. This was what he'd imagined since he was a boy. A house filled with friends and laughter. A family of his own making. Though he still held a smattering of jealousy that this family of his didn't include a wife and children, he refused to let that rob him of joy.

This was the Christmas he'd hoped for, and he'd gotten it. Maybe not tied up in a perfect ribbon, but with twine that kept his hope alive.

Cassandra began ushering people to the table once the food was ready. They started the slow procession into the dining room, Spencer carrying the platter of ham. Peter lingered behind, waving off Haley's help as he grabbed the basket of rolls and the glass tureen of cranberry sauce.

Everyone took their seats, and Peter was surprised to find himself sitting at the head of the table. As he didn't want to make a scene, he accepted the spot silently. Then, everyone turned to him expectantly.

Peter blinked, realizing they were waiting for him to say the prayer. He looked up the table to where Owen sat, having expected him or maybe even Andrew to say grace. But Owen gave him a nod, as though reminding him that Occasus was *his* house, and he was the true Varon, so it was *his* job.

Peter swallowed. "Uh . . ." He stared back at them all. "Let's pray, shall we?"

Immediately, they all held hands around the table.

Peter felt his brow pull together in bemused happiness. As he looked around the table at Spencer and Cassandra, Connor, Ava and Owen, Haley and Aaron, and Andrew and Aimee, he decided this was just right. He bowed his head and thanked God for the blessing of Christmas, family, friends, and the food before them.

Then, the meal erupted into gregarious conversation.

"You know," Aimee said mid-way through the meal, "I was looking back through the Rayne family records, and this gathering of ours is rather traditional."

Peter looked up from his plate. "It is?"

Aimee nodded. "It seems our families were very close—the Varons and the Raynes. In fact," she reached for her wine glass, "Matthias Varon, the founder of DeVerre, and Yvan Rayne, my three-times great-grandfather, were brothers-in-law."

Peter and Spencer shared a look, trying to figure out the relation.

"Wait," Cassandra jumped in. "So, Yvan was married to Matthias's sister?"

Aimee nodded, and Ava chimed in, "I was reading up about that too. Technically, that makes us cousins, though distantly."

"We're family, then?" Peter asked.

"Distantly," Ava repeated with a shrug.

The unexpected announcement sent a jolt of discomfort through Peter. He was suddenly very grateful that Connor Frossard had kept him from pursuing a relationship with Anna Lambert. He scrunched his nose at the thought, then shook it off.

"Huh." Peter smirked. "Does that make me your baby's uncle?"

"It makes you sixth cousins, once removed," Ava corrected.

Peter pursed his lips, unable to do the math.

Recognizing their family relation led to further discussion of their ancestry and the Varon/Rayne family ties over the years. It appeared that Aimee's family had been the right hand of the Varons within DeVerre. Their patriarchs were close friends by all accounts, Matthias often going to Yvan for advice or counsel. It was said that Yvan had done some great service for the Varons, though there was no record of just what that service was. But it had solidified their family trust for generations.

"Now that I'm aware of everything going on in DeVerre," Aimee said, "I assume this service had something to do with the spirit world."

"It would make sense," Ava agreed, then turned to Owen. "Do you remember that letter we were reading? The one from that Elizabeth woman?"

Peter and Spencer perked up.

Owen tipped his head in thought.

"She mentioned that she enclosed a package for Yvan," Ava reminded him. "As a thank you for his help."

At the prompting, Owen began to nod. "It had the symbol by the signature," he noted.

"Yes," Ava confirmed. "The one that matches Mom's necklace."

"This?" Aimee asked, pulling on the chain around her neck. A large gold signet hung from the end, a three-pronged symbol etched in the face, like a Y with an extra arm in the center. It looked vaguely reminiscent of a bird print.

At Ava's confirmation, Aimee pulled it from around her neck. "Here," she said, offering the necklace to her. "It's meant to be yours anyway. And perhaps Owen's Warden friends will recognize the symbol."

Ava took the necklace, slipping the chain over her head reverently.

Peter didn't know why, but something felt right about the moment, as though a prophecy were being fulfilled before his very eyes.

They finished their meal shortly after and began gathering in the living room, planning to play a card game, as was the Lambert family tradition. But Ava stepped over to Connor, at Peter's side, and handed him a package.

"I didn't buy it," she said. "So, no need to thank me. I just found it in her room and thought she'd want you to have it."

Connor unwrapped the gift, revealing a picture frame. Though Peter knew it wasn't polite, he tipped his head up to see. The photo was of a young Connor and Anna, perhaps around sixteen, maybe slightly younger. They were snuggled on a bench on the front porch of the Lambert house, his arm around her and her head on his shoulder. They looked blissfully happy, and Peter knew this was before Connor's father had ever threatened Anna. This was when the young man still had hope of marrying the girl he'd loved since they were in kindergarten.

Holding the picture tightly, Connor looked down at Ava. Neither said a word, but a silent understanding passed between them.

A twinge cut through Peter's stomach. Anna should be here. This moment, this should have been her at Connor's side. She should have gotten to enjoy this moment with her family—with their family.

"Hey," Peter called, drawing everyone's attention.

They turned to him, expectant.

"So, I know it's cold, and it's snowing, and it's Christmas, but . . ." Peter scanned the people around him, each of them bound together by one young woman. "I think we should go find Anna."

A single beat of silence met his suggestion.

Then, they were all in a flurry of agreement and rushing to get their coats.

Anticipation rose in Peter's chest as he bundled himself up. This was it, he told himself. He would stay out at the lake until he found Anna's ghost, even if he had to freeze through the night to do it.

Their large party trudged through the forest, helping one another over fallen trees and icy ridges. Despite the cold that turned their noses red within minutes, they laughed and enjoyed each other's company, excited by the prospect of finding their daughter, sister, and friend.

When they arrived at the lake, they decided to split up in pairs: Peter and Connor, Spencer and Cassandra, Aaron and Haley, Owen and Andrew, Ava and Aimee. As the Lambert parents couldn't see ghosts, they had to be with people who could. Ava, Aaron, and Haley had each become Heralds over the last month—Wielders who could see but not interact with ghosts.

They branched off, searching the forest, calling Anna's name. The forest was cold, the trees towering above them in the dark night. The waning gibbous moon overhead cast a dimmed glow as they searched.

After almost an hour of searching, Peter began to feel the first tremor of doubt as he shivered in the cold.

"Hey," Connor murmured as they wound toward the lake once more. "Just . . . If we don't find her—"

"Don't say that, man."

"Thank you," Connor said, pausing in the trees. "For everything. This last month has somehow been the worst month of my life and . . . and the best. Because of you."

Peter stalled in his walk. He looked up at his friend. "I haven't done anything," he said.

"You've been there," Connor replied with a shrug. "That's more than most people."

Peter didn't know what to say to that. He scratched the back of his head and worked to find words. But nothing came to him. Because what else was Peter supposed to have done over the last month? He wasn't going to give up on Anna. He wasn't going to leave Connor to his depression. He wasn't going to let them fail now that they'd removed the Druids from DeVerre. They had a life to live. And he was going to take care of the people around him because that's who he was.

"Merry Christmas," a soft voice said suddenly.

Peter and Connor froze.

Then, slowly, they turned to see a figure in the trees, her form washed in an ethereal gray. Wispy coils had slipped out of her ponytail to drift angelically around her face. She was as beautiful as ever in the most heart-wrenching way. Her puffer coat was ripped, and the knees of her jeans were muddy. Four jagged stripes scarred the left side of her face: one on her forehead, one across her temple, narrowly missing her eye, another under her high cheekbone, and the last tracing her jawline.

And still, her dark eyes held the brightest joy as Anna Lambert's ghost smiled at the two men.

"Sorry it took me so long to appear," Anna said, her voice like a gentle spring breeze to sweep away the icicles on their cold winter hearts. "Becoming a ghost is a more taxing process than you'd think."

Peter couldn't help his bemused laugh. He wanted to dart forward and hug her, but he knew he couldn't. He didn't doubt that Connor felt the strain of that truth even worse than he did, evidenced by the seemingly unconscious step the young man took toward her.

"You've been here the whole time?" Peter asked.

Anna nodded, her gaze darting to Connor. "Pretty much. I just didn't have the energy to make myself visible until now."

Peter looked at Connor. "A Christmas miracle?"

Connor didn't bother speculating but stepped forward to stand before the woman he loved. "We're gonna save you, Anna," he said.

Her brow furrowed, wrinkling the scar on her forehead. "I'm dead, Connor," she said weakly. "Honestly, I'm surprised I'm even a ghost. I'm ready to go. What's beyond this life . . . I know it's better than anything here."

Her lips tugged up fondly as she added, "Even you."

Connor shook his head. "It's not your time," he said. "Death isn't always the end. Sometimes, it's just another way to show God's power, entrusted to us." He raised his brow. "You taught me to believe in Him like that."

Anna hesitated, clearly unsure.

"You have more left to do here, Anna," Connor insisted. "Your work isn't finished, and we're going to bring you back so that you can finish it."

Looking past Connor's shoulder, Anna met Peter's stare as though asking for his unbiased opinion on the matter.

Knowing he couldn't be impartial if he tried, Peter shrugged. "You heard everything I said before, right?" he asked.

"Yes," she confirmed.

"Then you know," he gave her a dry grin, "DeVerre isn't DeVerre without you. We all need you back."

Anna took a deep breath. "Then," she looked up at Connor, her eyes glimmering with hope, "I guess you'd better figure out how to raise the dead."

Peter & Spencer will return
in book eight of Archives of the Warden

If you enjoyed this book,
consider leaving a review on Amazon or Goodreads

Places to follow my author journey:
Newsletter: vkdixon.substack.com
Instagram: @v.k.dixon
TikTok: @v.k.dixon

Also Available from V.K. Dixon

ARCHIVES OF THE WARDEN
Lake of Glass
Vault of Stone
The Raven's Cry
Veil of Mist
The Wolf's Howl
Of Spirit & Ether (Coming Spring 2026)
Book Seven (Coming Fall 2026)

WARRIORS & MAGES
Fire & Night
Sword & Shadow
Relics & Thrones

Peter's Nicknames for Spencer

& where they come from:

J.B. — Jessica "J.B." Fletcher, mystery writer and amateur sleuth *(Murder, She Wrote; television show)*

Sherlock — Sherlock Holmes, consulting detective with Scotland Yard *(Sherlock Holmes stories by Sir Arthur Conan Doyle)*

Poirot — Hercule Poirot, private investigator *(reoccurring character in Agatha Christie's mystery novels)*

Columbo — Lieutenant Columbo, police lieutenant and homicide detective *(Columbo; television show)*

Watson — Dr. John H. Watson, assistant and confidant of Sherlock Holmes *(Sherlock Holmes stories by Sir Arthur Conan Doyle)*

Matlock — Ben Matlock, defense attorney with a knack for solving the murders himself *(Matlock; television show)*

Frankly — Dr. Charles Frankly, ex-doctor turned private investigator *(Wenzel & Frankly serial by Peter and Spencer Collins)*

Glossary of Terms & Names

Aaron Lambert — *[Lam—bert]* — Middle of the three Lambert children; boyfriend of Haley Roux; mechanic; Herald Wielder

Advocate — Wielders who can interact with ghosts, tethering them as phantoms

Aimee Lambert — Mother of Ava, Aaron, and Anna; previous town librarian; descendant of Yvan Rayne

Anguis — *[An—gwis]* — German Wirehaired Pointer under the care of Peter and Spencer Collins-Varon

Alexander Frossard — *[Fros—sard]* — *aka 'Alex'* — Doctor in DeVerre; husband of Giana Frossard; father of Connor Frossard; Elder of the Druidic Faction in DeVerre; deceased

Allen Clement — *[Klem-ent]* — Father of Cassandra Clement; accountant; lives in Spokane

Anna Lambert — Youngest of the three Lambert children; bartender/waitress and artist; deceased

Arthur Wenzel — *[Wen—zuhl]* — Private investigator of the online serial *Wenzel & Frankly* written by Peter and Spencer Collins

Ava Bernard — Oldest of the three Lambert children; wife of Owen Bernard; town librarian; Herald Wielder

beast — A creature summoned from the spirit world to work on behalf of a Wielder

Benedict Varon — *[Vair—en]* — Eldest son of Gabriel Varon; father of the true Varon attributed with courage

Benjamin Powell — *aka 'Ben'* — Stepfather of Peter and Spencer Collins-Varon; second husband of Mallory Collins-Powell

Cassandra Clement — *[Kuh—san—druh]* — *aka 'Cass' or 'Cassie'* — Girlfriend of Spencer Collins-Varon; Vessel Wielder

Charles Frankly — Ex-doctor and private investigator of the online serial *Wenzel & Frankly* written by Peter and Spencer Collins

Cleric — Wielders who can interact with ghosts and summon beasts

Connor Frossard — Prior best friend of Anna Lambert; medical student; ex-Druid; Sage Wielder

David Collins — Late father of Peter and Spencer Collins; mechanic for the United States Navy

Debra Mercier — *aka 'Debbie'* — First cousin of Cassandra Clement's mother; descendant of the Sauveterre family; Druid

DeVerre, WA — *[Deh—Vair]* — Small town in northeastern Washington State

Diane Larkin — Late great-aunt of Peter and Spencer Collins-Varon; left the brothers her estate upon her death

Druids — *aka 'Children of Gaia'* — A cult of Wielders intent on releasing the spirit world upon the physical world

Gabriel Chapelle — *aka 'Gabe'* — Mortician; younger brother of Samuel Chapelle

Gabriel Varon — The first Varon

Gerard Alarie — Phantom from 1950s; once tethered to Occasus by Cassandra Clement

ghost — The lingering spirit of a dead Wielder with unfinished business in the physical world

Giana Frossard — *[Gee—ah—nah]* — *aka 'Gia'* — Friend of Anna Lambert; wife of Alexander Frossard; mother of Connor Frossard; Druid

Haley Roux — *[Rue]* — Fiancée of Aaron Lambert; friend and co-worker of Anna Lambert; Herald Wielder

Harmony, Saskatchewan — *[Suh—ska—chew—on]* — Original hometown of the founders of DeVerre, WA

Herald — Wielders who can see but not interact with ghosts

House of Occasus — *[Oh—kay—sus]* — Varon family estate; Diane Larkin's home, left to the Collins-Varon brothers

Isaac Clement — Older brother of Cassandra Clement

Jacob Howser — *aka 'Jake'* — Best friend to Isaac Clement; ex-boyfriend of Cassandra Clement

Julianne Clement — Mother of Cassandra Clement; cousin of Debra Mercier; descendant of the Sauveterre family

Juliet Chapelle — High school student; daughter of Samuel Chapelle

Mallory Collins-Powell — Mother of Peter and Spencer Collins-Varon; remarried to Benjamin Powell; lives in Norfolk, VA

Matthias Varon — Founder of DeVerre

Michael Mercier — *aka 'Mike'* — Husband of Debbie Mercier

Michael Varon — Great-grandson of Matthais Varon; last of the Varon line

Nex — German Wirehaired Pointer under the care of Peter and Spencer Collins-Varon

Owen Bernard — Husband of Ava Bernard; interim mayor of DeVerre; originally from Harmony, Saskatchewan; Sage Wielder

Peter Collins-Varon — *aka 'Pete'* — Writer; Sage Wielder; the true Varon of Benedict Varon's line

Phillip Collins — Grandfather of Peter and Spencer Collins-Varon; brother of Diane Larkin

phantom — A ghost that has been tethered to a specific location in the physical world

Porthaven, ME — Small, Warden-run town in the state of Maine

Sage — Wielders who can interact with ghosts, summon beasts, and wield the spirit world's essence (aka arcs or rifts)

Samuel Chapelle — *aka 'Sam'* — Reverend in DeVerre

Sandy Clement — Wife of Isaac Clement; sister-in-law of Cassandra Clement

Seraphine Frossard-Varon — Illegitimate daughter of Lloyd Frossard; secret wife of Michael Varon

Spectral — *aka 'spirit-being,' 'the kindred'* — A creature of the spirit world that attaches to a Vessel with unknown qualities and abilities

Spencer Collins-Varon — *aka 'Spence'* — Writer; Sage Wielder

spirit world — A parallel world that exists alongside the physical world

Thomas Garnier — *aka 'Tom'* — Marshal in DeVerre

true Varon — Leadership role with an inheritance of great power passed down through the Varon generations to the head of each primary bloodline, originating with Gabriel Varon's, the first Varon, three sons: Benedict, Edmond, and Henry

valravn — *[val-rav-en]* — Birdlike beast from the spirit world

Veil — Specific locations around the world where the boundary between the spirit world and the physical world is thin

Vessel — Wielders who can interact with ghosts, summon beasts, wield the spirit world's essence, and tether to Spectrals

the Warden — An organization of Wielders dedicated to protecting the spirit world from the control of the Druids

Wenzel & Frankly — Serial historical-fantasy blog written by Peter and Spencer Collins

Wielder — A human with the ability to wield the spirit world

William Larkin — *aka 'Liam'* — Late husband of Diane Larkin; writer; researcher of history and theology

Yvan Rayne — *[Ee-vahn Rain]* — Original record keeper in DeVerre; the Lambert siblings' ancestor

Acknowledgments

The Christmas season is my favorite time of year. I love the joy and beauty amidst the dark and frigid nights, the promise of renewed life within the death of nature, and the peace that can be found even in the hustle and bustle. I'd always wanted to write something light and pure fun surrounding this wonderful season, and I'm so glad I finally got to.

As always, I have to thank my husband for supporting me through this publishing endeavor.

Thank you to my betas: Anna, Alexandra, Lydia, Rachel, Rachelle, Serenity, and Stevie. I'm so thankful for your feedback and encouragement!

And most importantly, thank you to God, who is the very reason for this Christmas season. Your goodness, joy, and hope are why I love this holiday so much. I hope this little story brings your heart into the holiday for others.

About the Author

V. K. Dixon writes fantasy and romance novels filled with found family, lasting love, and unique magic. She believes that the extraordinary gives us a deeper desire for the things beyond us—the things of God.

www.ingramcontent.com/pod-product-compliance
Lightning Source LLC
Chambersburg PA
CBHW031532310726
48971CB00008B/2451